Unmasked

ALSO BY KATHLEEN LAWLESS

Taboo

Now available from Pocket Books

Unmasked

Kathleen
Lawless

POCKET BOOKS
New York London Toronto Sydney

POCKET BOOKS, a division of Simon & Schuster, Inc.
1230 Avenue of the Americas, New York, NY 10020

This book is a work of fiction. Names, characters, places and incidents are products of the author's imagination or are used fictitiously. Any resemblance to actual events or locales or persons, living or dead, is entirely coincidental.

ISBN 0-7394-4507-3

Manufactured in the United States of America

Dedicated to my parents, Robert and Diane,
an inspiring example of love at any age

And in memory of my grandfather, Jack Lawless,
who first planted the idea that I should write a book into my
impressionable twelve-year-old mind. He was right!

Unmasked

Chapter One

1899

"*The Grayson Estate,* Missus."

"It's huge!" Aurora Tremblay rested her elbows on the edge of the hot-air balloon's swaying wicker basket and leaned forward for a better look. From a sprawling mansion flanked by outbuildings amidst acres of formal gardens, to wooded copses, riding trails, a maze, and a pond, the estate below was far more grandiose than she'd expected. "Can you set down on the lawn over there?"

"I can try."

When the basket touched down on the manicured lawn of

the estate, Aurora hiked up her skirt with one hand, balanced her champagne glass in the other hand, and scrambled over the edge.

Once both feet landed on firm ground she straightened her hat and jacket and smoothed her skirt, as if such an entrance was an everyday occurrence. Since she'd cleverly avoided spilling even a drop of champagne, she tossed back her head and downed the contents of her glass. She'd need the extra fortification before she tackled the infamous Grayson Thorne, lord and master of the domain she had just breached.

The sound of applause momentarily caught her off guard, before she turned to her fan and made an exaggerated stage bow.

"Nicely done." The speaker was tall, broad of shoulder, and dark-haired. He appeared amused as he strolled toward her, a casual fluidity in his every step. Thorne? Or one of his henchmen?

If he thought to intimidate her, he'd need to do more than simply skim his eyes assessingly over her form. Except those dark, enigmatic eyes somehow managed to probe uncomfortably below the surface and ruffle her complacency. Why else would she suddenly feel as vulnerable as if she stood before him in her underpinnings, or less? As if he could see right through her well-rehearsed persona to the delicious secret longings that burned incessantly in her thoughts.

Ridiculous.

Impossible.

Not even the man she'd been married to had the slightest idea of her restless cravings, her innermost fantasies and desires.

"In fact," she said breezily, "it was quite the ride. Already I'm wondering what I might take on next."

"You make a habit of this type of thing?"

"I most certainly try." Was he laughing at her? Those firm lips curved upward in a way that seemed forced. Perhaps the man just wasn't accustomed to smiling very often. Surely a glower would be more at home on those handsome, ruggedly masculine features.

She dug into her reticule and pulled out a pristine new calling card, which she passed to him.

"Mrs. H. R. Tremblay," he read aloud. "Grand Adventuress." Now there was no mistaking the mockery in his tone and his eyes. "Just what does a grand adventuress do?"

"All manner of things." Drat, she sounded far too throaty, her words husky and breathless. A fact that did not escape the notice of the man before her. His reaction was subtle—a perceptible dilation of the pupils, a slight quickening of his breath as he acknowledged the intangible something that tautened between them. Almost as if invisible silken bonds slowly and surely twined them together.

Mad imaginings!

Aurora cleared her throat. "Could you please be so kind as to direct me to Grayson Thorne? He and I have an important matter to discuss."

His gaze swept her once more in that disconcerting fashion. Energy. Power. Magnetism. He had to be Thorne; for he exuded a fascinating combination of strength and raw sex that Aurora could not only see and smell and feel, but almost taste. She moistened her lips with her tongue, aware of the way he watched her slightest move, then matched it with one of his own.

She got the sense he was biding his time. Waiting for the right moment . . . To what—sweep her into his arms? Carry her into his lair? Now that would be an adventure. People spoke of the powerful Grayson Thorne with a hushed reverence and awe, and she was starting to see why.

"Your ride appears to have left without you."

Aurora swung about, aghast to see the balloon rising skyward. "He told me he would wait."

"The wind, it would seem, had different ideas."

How had Thorne gotten so close? One minute he'd been a safe distance from her, now he stood directly before her, very much larger than life. She sensed raw, unleashed power, barely glossed over and held in check by the dictates of polite society.

If he was a warrior, what battles did he fight? Inward? Outward? What secrets did he harbor behind those enigmatic dark eyes? What images haunted his sleep and invaded his dreams?

His presence was so powerful, she started when he touched her. He took her arm in a possessive, proprietarial manner and began to steer her in the direction of the mansion. "And thus it would appear that one adventure begets another, and you find yourself my unexpected guest."

"Do you entertain often?" She didn't want to antagonize

the man, simply state her business at the first opportunity, then be on her way.

"Sadly, no. With the exception of the next few days, of course."

"Oh?" Aurora allowed his hand to remain on her arm as she turned her attention toward the mansion, which, from the air, had appeared immense. Viewed up close it was just as imposing, sprawling in different directions.

"Indeed." They reached the front stairs just as a carriage rounded the bend and made its way up the drive toward them. When Aurora would have drawn back, Thorne's hold grew more insistent, a subtle pressure she felt radiate through her.

"The least you can do is come and help me greet my guests. And the very least I can do is refill your glass." He plucked the empty champagne glass from her hand and barked instructions to the bevy of household servants poised beneath the porte cochere to greet the carriage.

Aurora watched wide-eyed as trunk after trunk was unloaded with swift efficiency from inside the carriage.

The driver said, "The club members are following, sir. With the ladies."

"Very good." Grayson turned to his manservant. "Hudson, I'll leave you to see everyone gets comfortably settled."

"Certainly, sir."

"I've come at an inopportune time," Aurora said as Grayson marched her inside, across an immense marble-hued hallway with a curving antebellum staircase, to what was obviously his study. Dark wainscoting, a huge wooden desk, uncomfortable horsehair furniture. A true man's domain, as dark and forbidding as the man himself. The chair across from his desk proved as uncomfortable as it looked, clearly intended to discourage one from lingering in his lordship's presence.

"Extremely inopportune," he agreed. He opened a chilled bottle of champagne in a manner that suggested it was a frequent ritual, then made a production of refilling her glass. After delivering her drink, he poured himself a measure of whiskey and sprawled behind his desk.

Aurora took a sip. Business, she reminded herself. Ignore the unsettling effect he has on you. It's obviously well practiced and garners him results.

Her mind skipped off sideways, thinking of the result should the two of them suddenly be united in mutual effort. Or mutual ecstasy. Suddenly Aurora was far too warm, but she resisted the urge to slip out of her jacket, a move Thorne would no doubt interpret as weakness. He'd think he was ruffling her composure. Perhaps she should allow him that false impression, let him think he held the upper hand. "I didn't mean to crash your party."

"Well, you certainly intended to breach my privacy. Now that you're here, I'm afraid you'll find yourself dependent upon my good nature."

Aurora tilted her head and studied him from beneath lowered lashes, unable to resist baiting him as he baited her. "Do you even have one? A good nature, that is?"

"Come, come, Mrs. Tremblay. You have inveigled your way into my home and some very expensive French champagne. I'm neglecting my guests for you, so intriguing do I find your charming presence."

Another woman might fall back on her feminine wiles, flirting with him to pander to his ego. Aurora was not another woman. "Please don't."

He looked askance at her curt response.

She leaned forward. "Please don't attempt to flirt with me, as if I'm a guest whom you must make feel welcome. Simply hear me out, then dispatch me back to the city, posthaste."

He rose and refilled her glass although she'd barely touched its contents, his hand atop hers steadying the stemware. She felt the heat radiate from his fingertips and ignite her skin, a wildfire that rippled through her blood to pool in her feminine recesses.

"And just how do you propose I do that? Your rather irregular mode of arrival seems to have left you quite stranded."

Pointedly, she removed his hand from hers and stood as well. Much better to be eye to eye than have him loom over her. "Don't toy with me, Mr. Thorne. Simply bundle me into a carriage, and I'll be out of your way."

"Supposing I don't care to have you out of my way?"

"You have a houseful of guests to attend to."

"Strangers, most of the lot. Have you heard of the Rose and Thorn Club?"

"Of course." Anyone raised in the world of theater, as she had been, was well aware of the gentlemen's club, with its exclusivity and mystique. Having a club champion guaranteed the stage success of any actress. Thorne's father had been a founding member.

"Of course," Grayson echoed in slightly mocking tones. "Tell me, does Mr. Tremblay know what sort of adventure you've embarked upon?"

"I'm a widow," Aurora said.

"I wondered," Grayson said. "You have the look."

"What look?"

"The look of a woman who has been too long without a man."

"Ridicu—"

Grayson took the champagne glass from her fingers and set it down nearby. He ripped her hat from her head and tossed it aside, then dug his hands through her hair, tumbling it loose. "I like you mussed."

"Mr. Thorne."

"Mrs. Tremblay."

He intended to kiss her! Aurora couldn't still the jolt of excitement that accompanied the knowledge. She felt hot and liquid at the same time. Melting. Ready.

She swayed toward him, compelled by something too powerful to question. She knew only that she needed his kiss as badly as she needed to breathe. And that he felt the same.

His kiss was as masterful as he was. Sure. Strong. Knowing. Eliciting a heady response that danced through her blood and threatened to consume her.

Aurora caught his shoulders for support as waves of intense pleasure radiated through her. He was right. She *had* been too long without a man. And forever without one like him.

He drew back first, seeming far more in control than she.

"I take it you are the same Mrs. Tremblay who has been pestering my secretary for a meeting with me these past weeks."

Aurora nodded, still dizzy from his embrace. Her lips ached, yet begged for more. Her entire body throbbed and pulsated. How could she feel both sated and bereft? All from a single kiss? "I am indeed that same Mrs. Tremblay."

"Obviously you don't believe in taking no for an answer."

"Not when there's something I want this badly."

His coffee-colored eyes told her without words that he wanted her with equal fervor. The knowledge inflamed her.

"I'm rather like that myself. It can prove difficult."

Aurora knew they were speaking of two things at once, her desires versus his. "I manage quite nicely."

"So it would appear. Yet I fear, in this instance, you may find you've gotten more than you bargained for."

"Really, Mr. Thorne. When you refused to meet with me concerning the Gaslight Theater—"

He rose. "I have no intention of undertaking this discussion at this time. Come. I will show you to your room."

"My room? Surely you don't expect me to stay?"

"Oh, I think you'll stay. Seeing how there's something we both want. Badly."

"But—I have no things. No clothing or toiletries."

"Rest assured, I am more than able to see to your needs."

The promise in his words and his eyes was unmistakable.

All of her needs.

Aurora had the strong urge to bolt before she got too deeply embroiled. "Surely someone can fetch me back to the city."

"I'm afraid I don't have the staffing required to see you back to San Francisco."

"But your guests . . ."

"Will be as charmed to meet you as I have been, I'm quite sure." As they spoke he led the way upstairs to the end of the hall, where he opened the door to a sumptuous suite. "There is plenty of clothing in the armoire. You should manage to find something suitable."

She stepped past him and into what was most clearly not a guest room. It reeked of femininity in tones of pink and lavender. A multitude of flounces and frills draped a huge canopied bed that was drowned in pillows. Matching fabric swathed the windows. The domain of an absentee wife?

"Whose room is this?" Aurora advanced slowly, half-expecting that her surroundings might disappear into a cloud of smoke and mirrors.

Perhaps those years of make-believe, on stage and off, had finally taken their toll. Perhaps she wasn't capable of separating fantasy from reality, even though she no longer had to act on stage for a living. Once she'd married Hubert, it wasn't considered seemly to pursue her career, he'd said. Was that when her grown-up longings and fantasies had been born, with time on her hands and little to amuse herself save her imagination?

On the far side of the room near the fireplace, framed photos lured her to a side table. Thorne stood stiffly, legs apart, hands clasped behind his back as she picked up a picture and studied it in the fading afternoon light.

"This is my mother's room. She hasn't been here in quite some time."

Aurora spun about to face her host, recognizing the shadow. The lonely young boy awaiting the return of his beautiful and famous mother. "Celeste Grayson is your mother."

"Excellent deductive powers, Mrs. Tremblay."

"The Gaslight Theater is where she first got her big break."

Just like that, Grayson's face shut down, devoid of all expression. "I see you've researched the property."

Aurora's eyes remained on his. "I'm also aware that your father's body was discovered on the site."

"Very good, Mrs. Tremblay. Who knows what other interesting snippets you might discover over the next three days?"

What, indeed?

RANDALL AMES STROLLED INTO Grayson's study a short time later. "Who's the knockout redhead I saw you escorting upstairs?"

"You mean, Mrs. H. R. Tremblay, Grand Adventuress?" Gray said mockingly, flipping the calling card to his secretary.

Randall caught the card deftly, frowning as he read it. "Grand Adventuress? Likely more talk than action. Why does the name sound familiar?"

"She's been hounding you for a meeting with me these past weeks."

"Ah, yes. Aurora Tremblay. The one you told me to get rid of."

"A task at which it would appear you failed miserably."

"Someone who doesn't take no for an answer, is she?

Forgive me, but isn't tenacity one of those character traits you most admire?"

"Only when it suits me," Gray said.

"So send her on her way."

"Not until I know exactly who and what she's all about."

"Doesn't she have designs on the theater?"

"Perhaps," Gray said, recalling the delectable way she felt in his arms, her response to his impulsive kiss. He'd thought to repel her with his advances, yet the exact opposite had happened—and he wasn't accustomed to being so wrong in his judgment of people. That alone was enough to intrigue him.

"The rooms have all been assigned. Where are you going to put her?"

"She's in Celeste's room."

Randall raised a brow. "In your wing. How very convenient."

"At least that way I'll be able to keep a close eye on her. I don't need any more unpleasant surprises."

"What's Beau been up to now?"

"His usual. Making promises he has no intention of keeping."

"Chip off the old block that way, isn't he?"

"He does seem to favor his mother."

Randall laughed aloud. "Last I heard, Celeste was your mother, as well."

Gray shot him a sharp look. "I'll thank you not to remind me."

* * *

HARDLY THE AUSPICIOUS AUDIENCE she had set out to obtain with Grayson Thorne, but it was a start, Aurora thought as she made a more leisurely perusal of the room. To think that Celeste Grayson was Thorne's mother. The woman who was not only a legend in the theater world, but equally well known for her legion of lovers.

Aurora had had a bit part onstage with the woman once. Celeste wouldn't remember her, but it was an experience Aurora had never forgotten. This room showed a different side of the woman Aurora remembered. Her love of books, her passion for art, along with many other creature comforts. Not to mention clothing, for the armoire door was nearly bursting off its hinges. Aurora pulled out a simple day shift in spring tones and held it against her. It smelled faintly of a seductive floral scent. So Grayson expected her to take up residence in his mother's room and help herself to his mother's clothes, did he? Quite a cheek.

Aurora had no intention of sitting about meekly, waiting to be summoned. She pushed aside the curtains and took in the surrounding grounds. She caught a glimpse of the pond in the distance, beyond the formal rose garden and arbor, past the maze.

She had need of Grayson. Rather, she corrected herself quickly, she needed what he had—the Gaslight Theater. And she was quite certain that she'd be able to convince him of the merit of her plans. He'd soon find she wasn't easily swayed from her goals.

The manor house was unexpectedly quiet as she made her way downstairs. Perhaps Grayson's guests had been delayed, and the staff was busy with behind-the-scenes preparations.

Once outside, Aurora faced a quandary. The maze . . . the sculpture gardens . . . the summerhouse . . . the pond . . . Each one beckoned, promising an adventure.

"If you're looking for Gray, he's in the summerhouse." A fair-haired youth rose from the depths of a wicker chair in the shadows of the porch.

"And the summerhouse is . . . ?"

"That way," the young man said, pointing and extending his hand in one lazy movement. "I'm Gray's brother, Beau."

"Aurora Tremblay," she said, taking his proffered hand. The young man was slender, almost pretty, and she sensed weakness in both his handshake and his personality, reminding her of her late husband. Perhaps the younger brother was simply spoiled. Whatever the cause, she saw no evidence of Grayson's strength in his sibling.

"You one of the actresses, then?"

"I've been onstage a time or two."

"Gray didn't want to host the party, you know. Julian badgered him into it. On account of it was Gray's father's turn."

"I see." Aurora doubted Grayson was easily badgered into anything, so he must have his own agenda. Something to do with his father's death and his newly inherited membership in the exclusive Rose and Thorn, perhaps. "I think I'll go and see if I can beg a minute of his time."

Grayson's estate proved as remarkable as the man himself. The pathway she followed was flanked by a verdant broadleaf hedge with a profusion of colorful blooms, whose fragrance spiked the air with a sweet-smelling perfume. Jasmine twined about the overhead archway, shielding her from the late-afternoon sun and adding its own exotic fragrance.

Aurora stooped and picked up a bright orange bloom from the ground. As she tucked it behind one ear, she realized she had neglected to tidy her hair after Grayson had run his hands through it. Or did she just not wish to erase the memory of his touch? She couldn't pretend she hadn't enjoyed the excitement of being in his arms, of experiencing his kiss. Even now a thrill chased through her, clear to the tips of her fingers and the soles of her feet.

Glancing about, she suddenly felt younger and more carefree than she had in years. So much responsibility had come her way, especially after her marriage, as Hubert's waning health and weak character had forced her to be the strong one of the couple.

No wonder she found herself drawn to Grayson Thorne. How could she resist a man whose physical strength paired effortlessly with strength of character? A man who wouldn't allow himself to be pushed or bullied, any more than she did. Whose power could enhance without quelling hers if she played her cards correctly. Somehow she needed to convince him that a partnership was in their mutual interests.

She reached the charming open-air summerhouse, disappointed to find no sign of her host. Did she secretly hope that here, in a heavy silence broken only by the trill of birdsong, he'd pull her into his arms and kiss her again? Open-air coupling, the thrill of the forbidden—only one of the many sexual adventures hinted at in Grayson's knowing gaze. Aurora shivered at the delicious direction of her thoughts. No matter that her fantasies would never come to fruition; they fed her soul and nurtured her adventurous spirit.

Aurora climbed the three steps to the cool, sweet-smelling interior, an idyllic mix of indoors and out with its encroaching greenery, casual wicker furniture, and slatted, half-open ceiling, intended more for shade than privacy. She stretched out upon a wicker settee and sank several inches into an overstuffed feather mattress. Dreamily, she gazed up at the ceiling. She'd just settle in here for a bit and see if Grayson showed up.

SHE AWOKE AT DUSK, blinking herself awake, hungry and totally disoriented. In the west she could see the last fading pink fingers of the sunset, backlit by a faint golden glow.

She stirred and sat up. How odd. She didn't recall there being a blanket here when she first lay down, but she was cozily warm beneath one now. She touched it and discovered it was not a blanket at all, but a black velvet cloak. And lying on the pillow, next to the faint indentation from her head, was a matching velvet mask.

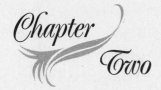

Chapter Two

Aurora looked around, wondering if she was alone in the summerhouse. The building's corners were deeply shadowed, dark enough to keep secret the presence of another. A faint summer breeze rustled the broadleaf shrubs that stood sentry at the building's entrance.

In the distance she heard a faint, melodious tinkle, the haunting melody of chimes moving with the breeze. As their song slowly faded to nothing in the still air, Aurora heard only the rise and fall of her own breath. Her heart sounded crashingly loud beneath her ribs as she swung her legs over the side of the settee and stroked the black velvet mask.

Would all the guests be wearing them? Somehow she suspected that they would. And no one would know who anyone else was. Such an intriguing thought—total freedom to be whoever, whatever she wanted. A queen. A pharaoh. A courtesan. A powerful woman capable of driving a man to distraction. She fondled the plush texture, rasped her nail across the eye cutouts, twined the satin ties around her forefinger. Finally, she gave in to temptation. She stood and positioned the mask across her features.

"Allow me."

Aurora gasped as strong, capable hands took over for hers, securing the ties behind her head. Where had he come from? Had a stranger lingered in the shadows, watching her sleep, influencing her dreams? For she'd woken with a heavy throbbing need between her legs. Her skin prickled all over with supersensitivity, nerve endings tingling with exposure to something new and exciting in the air.

Like the man who stood behind her. His warm breath stirred her hair and pinpricks of awareness licked across her scalp, heightened by the brush of his fingers. He pushed her hair aside and touched his lips to her sensitive nape. Aurora trembled in reaction.

"Grayson?"

Silently he moved to stand before her, a dark phantom in a matching mask and cloak. "No names," he said, his voice as muffled and indistinguishable as the dusk. "You need the cloak as well."

With a flourish, he settled the garment across her shoulders. As he secured the toggle fastenings, the backs of his knuckles brushed her breasts in delicious slow motion. Throbbing heat simmered through her and she bit her lower lip, awash in the flood of sensation. If the accidental brush of his hands could stir her so, what would happen if he touched her with deliberate, knowing intent?

She trembled again and restrained herself from reaching for him. "Why the disguise?" she asked, when she finally rediscovered her voice.

"Club tradition."

"The world's a stage, and we the players?"

"That seems the way of things. Come, I'll escort you safely back to the house."

Aurora swallowed her disappointment. Clearly he had no intention of seducing her. "I can make my own way, thank you."

"I wouldn't."

Her gaze found his. They had to be Grayson's eyes; she wouldn't respond thus to any other. "And why is that?"

"The grounds appear entirely different at night; it's easy to lose one's way. And a woman alone would be considered . . ."

"Would be considered what?"

"To be seeking company."

"That's not the case with me." *I crave the company of only one.*

"Then I suggest you accept my kind offer."

"I am not convinced it stems purely from kindness."

Strong white teeth flashed in a wolfish smile. Grayson's smile. "Selfish, then."

"I find that a far more believable motive."

"Ssshhhh." His fingers on her lips rendered her silent as he tugged her into the concealing shadows of the room's deepest corner. So intent was she on savoring the feel of him next to her, she barely heard the soft feminine gurgle of a woman's laughter. The sound was echoed by the low, throaty rumble of a man's voice as the couple scampered up the steps. Once inside, faint moonlight backlit the way two bodies merged into one, drew apart briefly, then reunited.

Aurora tensed as the breeze played with the unmistakable moan of a woman aroused, then the harsher indrawn breath of the male preparing to mate.

She couldn't possibly remain there.

Yet when she tried to move, she found herself imprisoned against the solid, masculine form of her companion . . . and lost all desire to move.

She was aware of hardened muscles, coiled strength, every lean and hard male inch of him. Could he be naked beneath the concealing cloak?

She instantly felt stiflingly hot beneath her own cloak. Her skin prickled and beaded with moisture in the most intimate of places. The tops of her thighs, the backs of her knees, the valley between her breasts. She shifted as a fiery restlessness shot through her.

And when her companion clasped her closer still, settled her against him and into him, her blood sang with the rightness of the way she nested with him.

How well they fit together, Aurora thought as she lifted her face toward his. She already knew their lips fit as well as their bodies. While she was tall for a woman, her companion was the perfect height alongside her. Tall enough to shelter and protect her should the need arise, but not too tall that he loomed threateningly over her, or that his height made her uncomfortable.

His strong legs moved against hers, more than capable of supporting her weight should she feel weak. His warm breath fanned her face, and her heart sped up. She could see his fathomless dark eyes through the holes in his mask, see the intriguing shape of his lips, so close to her own. Kissably close.

Across the room, the settee upon which she had so recently reclined became the destination of the two clandestine lovers. Cloaks rustled and afforded the occasional glimpse of bare skin, alabaster white limbs against midnight velvet.

Moans mingled with throaty murmurs as the lovers twined and coupled. Mouth to mouth, breast to chest, then mouth to breast. Aurora buried her face against the broad, capable chest of her companion. His arms enfolded her, promised to shield her.

From what? Aurora wondered. From herself?

For her breath quickened in tandem with that of the trysting couple, who were joined in nature's most primal dance.

Her phantom's breathing deepened. His hands sifted through her hair as if unable to still themselves, and the orange bloom dropped to her feet. She felt his muscles tense as he pressed her closer, felt his cock thicken and lengthen against her. She nearly gasped aloud at the power of her response, but his lips captured hers, silenced her. Consumed her.

His hands shifted from her hair to chart the length of her spine, finding and shaping her feminine curves the way his lips learned the secrets of her mouth. Her breasts tingled, her nipples budded, then pouted with neglect when he failed to pay them the much-needed attention. She felt his heat beneath the cloak and pushed the garment aside to unfasten his shirt, touching his bare chest the way she longed to be touched.

The railing of the building was behind her, supporting her weight as he leaned into her, every inch of him flush with every inch of her, the sensation through their cloaks as powerful as if they wore nothing at all.

The writhing couple across the room ceased to exist as her partner's pelvis locked with hers, rocking in the most intimate promise of all. As his clever fingers plucked her nipples through the fine silk of her favorite blouse, she bit her lower lip to prevent her cry of pleasure and swallowed a further cry of frustration at her growing need for release.

He seemed to sense her every need. Silently, he shifted her till she balanced upon the railing, her legs straddling his midsection, hugging his waist. Smoothly he pushed her skirt aside.

She felt the cool night air whisper through the delicate lawn of her pantalettes. Seconds later, his knowing fingers found the damp heat of her slit. Deftly he teased the secret, burning woman part of her.

A rush of female pleasure spilled from her, dampening her underthings along with his fingers. He gave a low, approving murmur only she could hear as he located the throbbing nub that craved his touch more than life itself. As he continued to tease and torture, Aurora rocked against him, her lower lip caught in her teeth as the sensations built in intensity, and release continued to elude her.

Vaguely she grew aware of a flurry of movement from nearby. Footfalls on the steps signaled they were now alone. She heard frantic, desperate panting and traced the source to herself.

"I want—" Aurora stopped, having no idea what it was she burned for.

"Whatever you want." His growled words sounded as if they were ripped from his throat.

"I want you." The audacity of her words might have shocked her in another time or place, but not now. Nor did they stop her from rubbing against him in a far more intimate fashion than anything she had ever done during her marriage.

That wolfish, satisfied, very male grin reappeared. "Patience, my lovely."

Without unseating her, he slipped her pantalettes down one leg at a time. Then he knelt before her, her legs resting on his shoulders, securing her balance.

Moist, hot, hungry kisses branded her inner thighs and marked her as his. Aurora gasped aloud and tightened her grip on the railing beneath her. His chin was peppered with the faint stubble of whiskers, rubbing suggestively against the softness of her softest skin. A deliciously arousing sensation continued to build as he ran his tongue from her stocking top to the triangular juncture of her womanhood.

"You like that, mmmmm?" he murmured against her.

Aurora released a long, pent-up sigh of agreement. The sigh turned into a gasp when his lips touched her most intimate inner sanctum, dampening already-moist recesses with new desire. Aurora gasped again as he traced her shape with his tongue, discovering all her secrets.

"Your clit is so hard—begging for my kiss."

As he put words to action and lapped at the pearl of her womanhood, Aurora's world exploded into a white-hot chasm of light. Barely had one tremor started to subside when it was heightened by another, followed by a third. His tongue gentled, soothing her, clearly enjoying the way the rippling aftershocks slowly eased to a gentle internal pulsing.

"You taste delicious. The unmistakable flavor of a woman well and truly sated." His voice rang with satisfaction as he steadied her and rose to his feet.

"I still want you." Aurora didn't even recognize the seductive, husky tone of her own voice.

"In you?"

"You were right," Aurora whispered against his neck. "I've been too long without a man."

He captured her lips with his own and sipped the words as she spoke, savored them and went back for more.

She reached between them to stroke the hot, turgid length of his cock through his trousers. He was so big. So hard. Never had she known such need, such craving, such sexual greed.

He freed his cock, then brought the tip of his shaft to her entranceway, teasing the ginger-colored curls. Gently he probed for admittance, slid easily inside her slickness, then withdrew before sliding in farther.

Aurora moaned aloud at the exquisite sensation of him filling her. She had been empty for so long. Forever. Now, finally, she understood how it felt to be well and truly mated to someone.

His breathing grew harsh as he increased the pace of his actions. Aurora could see the pale glimmer of his shaft as he pulled nearly all the way out, then buried himself deep inside her. More heat, more bright light, more moisture prefaced a new, intense pressure from somewhere deep within.

Her inner muscles clenched, then released, then clenched again, teasing him the way he had teased her earlier. He groaned, and his movements quickened in tandem with hers. The pressure built to an unbearable pitch until her orgasm burst, together with his. Aurora screamed, then trembled with the rippling aftermath. She had no idea how long he held her; she only knew it was torture to let go.

The intrusion of that thought was enough to catapult her into action, into her clothing and anxious to be on her way. She never had trouble letting go. An adventuress prided herself on being able to move swiftly and easily from one adventure to the next, without the burden of forming unnecessary attachments.

She didn't say a word as they made their way through the silken night air to the mansion, and neither did her companion. She was careful not to touch him or to brush against him, although she did occasionally sneak a sideways glance.

Part of her needed to know if her phantom lover was indeed Grayson. The other part told her to leave it be, to accept the evening's interlude as a lovely and unexpected gift.

At the front door, her masked mystery man turned to her

and pressed her hand between both of his. "I will bid you farewell. And commend the fact that you don't feel compelled to chatter incessantly, as do most women."

Aurora's gaze met his. "In case it had escaped your notice, I am hardly most women."

It was a most worthy exit line, delivered with just the right amount of fire and ice.

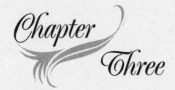

Chapter Three

Aurora woke early and went out onto the balcony, just as the first brilliant colors of the dawn stained the horizon. She took a breath and leaned against the railing, marveling at the splendor unfolding before her. The energy of dawn's arrival was a powerful force she felt in every fiber of her being.

Had last night in the summerhouse been real or just part of a long, wonderful dream? Blessed with an active imagination, Aurora had spent much of her youth in fanciful imagined places with imaginary playmates. But the satisfyingly tender pull between her legs told her that last night had been very real indeed. So did the faint red love bites on her inner thighs that she discovered when she washed.

She trailed her fingers across the sensitive crease at the top of her thighs, recalling the heat of Grayson's lips, Grayson's tongue. The memory fueled fresh desire. Dear Lord, she was becoming as wanton as a courtesan, one tumble with the man only whetting her appetite for more. This, then, was the all-consuming passion that she'd always dismissed as wildly exaggerated talk. For her marriage bed had provided naught but embarrassment and failure for her and Hubert till they stopped trying.

Still, if Grayson Thorne had thought to distract her from her goal by seduction, he would be sorely disappointed.

Her movements faltered.

If Grayson Thorne had been last evening's masked lover.

Hardly the type of subject one could comfortably broach over the breakfast table the next day.

"By the way, superb shagging last night. That *was* you down in the summerhouse, wasn't it?"

Well, she'd simply pretend nothing happened. After all those years of making her living onstage, this role ought to be a breeze.

And perhaps he didn't even know it was her.

Aurora knew she was grasping at straws—not only had he watched her sleep, her red hair gave her away every time. Mask or no mask, her lover knew exactly whom he had partnered with.

Aurora refused to allow anyone an unfair advantage over her, so she'd simply make sure she leveled things between herself and Grayson. The prospect could be good fun.

The house was silent, and she moved quietly to dress, pleased to discover that not all of Celeste's clothing was of the highly dramatic style of an actress. She selected a tailored skirt and gauzy blouse in rich cinnamon tones.

Anticipation made her clumsy as she pinned up her hair, and it took longer than usual to subdue her fiery curls into a reasonable knot atop her head. The library was her destination, and it was deserted at this early hour, as she had hoped. She stepped inside, pulled the door shut behind her, and stood looking her fill in the morning half-light.

Shelf after shelf crammed with books from floor to ceiling beckoned, a rainbow of spines. Aurora couldn't imagine living in the midst of such bounty; even the smell was intoxicating. Aged leather, glue, heavy paper . . .

Books had been a rare and highly prized commodity when she was young. The one book she had owned as a child had been lost in one of their many moves, forcing Aurora to live in a world of her own invention. Later, as more books became available to her, Aurora read as much as she was able, every chance she got. Reading fueled her imagination and whetted her appetite for real adventures.

She lit the fire, already laid in the grate, and it lent the room an even cosier air as it crackled to life. After Aurora had made her decision and settled on *Black Beauty,* she went in search of some tea.

"You're up early, dearie," remarked the plump and pleasant woman in the kitchen, up to her elbows in flour and raw dough.

"I was hoping to beg a cup of tea," Aurora said.

"Easy as a wink." The woman whisked the flour from her chubby arms, then poured Aurora a cup of tea from the enamel pot on the back of the stove. "Skinny things, you theater folk. I'll make you some toast to keep you going till breakfast."

"I'm fine, really."

The cook, who introduced herself as Mrs. Blossom, overrode Aurora's objections, toasted her some thick-sliced homemade scone bread, which she slathered generously with butter and preserves, then shooed Aurora out of the kitchen.

Immersed in a world other than her own, pleasantly full from the tea and toast, cosy warm and half-asleep before the fire, it took a few moments before Aurora realized that the sound intruding into her consciousness was the opening of the library door. She was no longer alone.

Aurora tensed at the sound of brisk male strides on the far side of the room, and felt *his* presence as surely as if he'd brushed against her. Her skin prickled in awareness, flushed with heat and excitement. How could that possibly be, just from being in the same room as he?

She heard the sound of papers rustling. Perhaps he'd find what he sought and leave without ever knowing she was here. Yet surely he noticed that the fire had been lit. Shrinking from notice had never been Aurora's style, and she set her book down, rose from behind the cover of the wing chair's bulk, and turned to face her host.

"Good morning, Grayson."

She'd thought to catch him off guard, but he didn't even spare her a glance.

"Aurora. You've found my favorite room, I see." He looked past her to her empty dishes. "And my favorite tea and toast."

"Mrs. Blossom deemed me too skinny."

"Mrs. Blossom deems everyone too skinny. Save Mr. Blossom, whom she is forever chiding for his portly shape, even as she feeds him far too well."

"This room is truly amazing."

"Books were my grandfather's passion. Or his excuse to hide away, much to the annoyance of my grandmother. I think that's why the grounds are so lavish: She needed a hobby, as well."

"They've certainly left behind an amazing legacy for future generations."

"Assuming there will be future generations."

Didn't all men seek an heir? She pointed to a portrait on the far wall, a stern and older version of Grayson. "Is that your grandfather?"

"It is."

"Your father's father?"

"My mother's. Jeremy Grayson."

So the estate had come to him through his mother.

Silent tension spun her mischief as they faced each other.

"I watched the sunrise this morning," Aurora said in a rush to fill the silence.

"Of course you did," Grayson said. "Aurora is the Roman version of Eos. Morning mother of the sun."

Aurora gasped in surprise. "How did you know that?"

"I believe in knowing all I can about people I'm about to come into contact with."

"You didn't know for certain we would ever meet."

"Some things are inevitable."

Emboldened, Aurora continued, "And last night's sunset, as viewed from the summerhouse. Was it not equally magnificent?" Would he admit to having been there with her?

"I'm afraid I was far too . . . busy last evening to enjoy the sunset."

"A pity," Aurora said. "You ought to try and take it in this evening."

"Come here. Allow me to show you something which I think you'll find of interest."

He led her to a corner table, where a thick volume lay open, almost as if awaiting their approach. Its pristine, empty white pages seemed out of place in this room where literature and family history reigned supreme.

"There are no words," Aurora said. "What's the point of a blank book?"

"Impulsive by nature, you judge too quickly. Look again."

Aurora did, and felt foolish. "Oh." She reached to touch, then turned to him for permission. "May I?"

Grayson stood directly behind her, his hands atop hers guiding her hesitant fingers onto the page before her. She shivered in reaction to Grayson's nearness as she found the raised bumps of Braille beneath her fingertips. Grayson's slightest touch thrilled her; even the caress of his gaze caused a powerful surge of desire.

He stood so close behind her that she could feel his warm breath stirring the tiny curls tickling the back of her neck. His arms enfolded her in an embrace that was at once intimate and circumspect. He leaned in as his hands guided her fingers along the page, his lips all but grazing her ear as he spoke.

It took a second for her to realize he was reading aloud from the text beneath their fingers. A lyrical description of a man's first glimpse of a beautiful woman.

"You read Braille?"

"Sadly, no. My grandmother did, after her sight failed. But I did manage to learn that passage by heart when I was younger. Finally, I think I truly understand how the young man must have felt." As he spoke, Grayson's hands slid upward to her wrists, then slowly, lingeringly, made the journey to her elbow. The thin fabric of her blouse proved no impediment for the warmth of his skin on hers or the heat generated by his nearness.

When she sensed he was about to step away from her, Aurora caught his hands in hers and raised them to her midriff. It became her turn to chart the movement, as slowly, deliberately, she guided his hands upward from her rib cage to the soft and waiting curve of her breasts.

She felt the sharpness of his indrawn breath as he gauged the sureness with which she encouraged him, the boldness of her actions shocking them both.

She turned her head ever so slightly, nuzzled her vulnerable neck against his lips. "Pretend I'm Braille."

"Reading Braille was never like this." His palms cupped her heavy, needful breasts, and her nipples pebbled in response.

Aurora sighed softly in relief. How desperately she had needed his touch. The rush of heat from her loins intensified as his lips grazed her neck, and he tongued the sensitive curve from ear to shoulder.

Aurora quivered. His hands slid from her breasts to her hips in a slow, provocative motion, molding her shape and pulling her hips back against his.

She leaned in more fully, enjoying the fullness of heavy limbs, the way their two bodies flowed into one. His obvious state of arousal, which he made no effort to hide.

With a provocative side-to-side motion, she rubbed her bottom against him, gratified to hear the sudden catch of his breath. She reached up and around behind her to tangle her fingers through his thick, dark hair before tracing the contours of his strong, masculine features. Cheekbones. Jaw. Hot and hungry lips.

She turned in his arms, and as she tilted her head in invitation, those hot and hungry lips found hers. She groaned aloud at the sheer deliciousness of his kiss. His greedy tongue ravished hers, engaged it in a mating ritual as old as time. Aurora clung to him, unable to get enough of him. Ever.

He broke the kiss first and leaned against her, his hands clasping her face, his forehead resting lightly against hers. His breath ran fast and furious as he fought for self-control.

"Last night. In the summerhouse. That was you," she said.

"Don't take anything that happens this weekend at face value. The Rose and Thorn is all about anonymity. Faceless coupling. Hence the masks."

"The mask reveals as much as it conceals."

Grayson started at her words, making Aurora wonder just

what he was trying to conceal. Was he hiding from her? Or from himself? "Perhaps I am the mirror, reflecting back that which you don't care to acknowledge."

"Deep thoughts from one so young," he said lightly.

"Some of us are born old. Born in wisdom. Or in shame."

"Let me remind you, this week's end is one long party. Tonight each guest will find his or her mate clad in the identical color of cloak."

She tilted her head. "Make certain then that you and I are dressed alike."

"You dare to dictate?"

"You dare to control." She felt the beginning of him releasing her, pretending an indifference she knew he was far from feeling.

"You're free to leave anytime the games become too much for you."

"You challenged me to stay."

"And now I challenge you to play."

"I accept your challenge. And match it with one of my own." She'd surprised him again with her boldness. It felt good.

"What's that?"

"I want my meeting with you."

"It shall be yours—provided you stay the weekend."

"Why are you doing this? Why are you bothering with this club, these people? Their cloak-and-dagger games in the dark? What possible interest do you have in their world of make-believe?"

He stepped back, his manner as distant as if they had not

just been locked in a passionate embrace. "My interest is my own. And none of your concern."

Grayson was very wrong, Aurora thought as she watched him take his leave. Everything about Grayson Thorne had become her concern.

"IT APPEARS THAT ALL is here and accounted for, Gray," Randall said, as he helped himself to toast and coffee and joined Grayson at the massive walnut dining table. "I must say, those club members have more paraphernalia than what the actresses brought along for their performances."

"Don't forget, everything that you see here this weekend is all part of a performance. Every tiny, insignificant-appearing nuance. Nothing is real."

"Explain to me again just why you're upsetting your well-ordered life in this fashion."

"I'm hosting the party in my father's memory."

Randall shook his head. "This is me you're talking to, Gray. I know your father started the club, with Julian's prompting, I suspect."

Gray fell silent. He knew exactly why his father had started the club. What he didn't yet know was what his father had been doing inside the Gaslight Theater the night he died. Although little pieces of his father had been dying for years, every time Celeste flaunted one of her many lovers in his face, Gray knew his father would *never* have chosen suicide.

His parents' ongoing argument had grown tiresome over the years. Celeste truly believed that her infidelity was not her fault. Men saw her onstage and wanted her, and she hadn't the strength to refuse them. His father had forgiven her and taken her back countless times. But Gray saw the ultimate cost, and had vowed never to fall in love, victim to a woman's charms and beauty.

He understood, as well, Jonathan's rationale for establishing the club. It was his turnabout on Celeste. The club offered wealthy older theater patrons the chance to consort with a variety of young, attractive partners, all in the guise of creativity. A living play in which they all had starring roles.

"Excuse me, sir."

Gray glanced up to see his butler standing before him wringing his hands. "What is it, Hudson?"

"The young auburn-haired woman, sir. She was seen heading in the direction of the pond."

"Bloody hell," Gray said as he rose. He still hadn't quite caught his balance from his early-morning encounter with Aurora in the library; she was totally unpredictable. "Why can't she sleep the day away like the rest of the guests?"

"Yes, sir. And the staff, sir."

"What about the staff?"

"They are uncertain of their role in the weekend festivities, Mr. Thorne."

"The guests are more than capable of amusing themselves. Just instruct the staff to be unobtrusive, pitch in where asked, and see to the guests' comfort. Anything else?"

Hudson wrung his hands again, and Gray softened. "I know it's disruptive having this lot underfoot. But it's only for three days."

"Still," Hudson said, "it's quite the goings-on."

"Yes, man. Well, do your best," Gray said.

Randall laughed aloud as the fellow took his leave. "You are the only employer I know who actually allows his servants to tell him how they think things ought to be handled."

"Good help is hard to find. And I'd watch my tongue if I were you, or you might find yourself seeking new employment in the bargain."

Randall rose lazily. "Whether you like to admit it or not, you need me, Gray. No one else could put up with you."

"I'm afraid you may be correct on that score. Now if you'll excuse me, I'd best see to the safety of our errant guest."

Chapter Four

Aurora came upon the pond suddenly, just as she despaired of ever finding it. Having seen the estate from the air and from the vantage point of her verandah, she'd gotten a good overview of the layout—but things looked entirely different from the ground. Pathways wandered and meandered. Foliage disguised certain key signposts, including the pond itself, where the watercourse was edged by weeping willows, their branches sweeping low into the water. Equally well hidden was a shade-dappled nook with a bench and a dock. And wonder of wonders, tugging playfully at her moorings, was a white rowboat.

The pond stretched before her, much larger than it had appeared from the air, home to a charming wooden gazebo in the center. Not a whisper of breeze marred the pond's mirror-like surface. The willow branches' reflection made it nigh impossible to tell where the shore ended and the water began, despite the way bullrushes poked their dark, reedy heads at the far end.

Nearby, the rowboat beckoned, entirely too much of a temptation.

"Who cares if I've not boated before?" Aurora's voice echoed across the pond. "I'd never ballooned before yesterday, either."

From the wood-planked docking she edged forward, gathered her skirt in one hand, and clambered gingerly aboard. The boat seesawed slightly as she plunked herself on the center wooden seat.

One end of the boat was pointed, while the other end was square. She'd sit with her back to the pointy end, she decided, as she lifted the oars from the bottom of the boat and made sure they were fixed securely into their oarlocks.

Wouldn't boating make a terrific moving picture? She'd already seen a locomotive and a moving wagon; why not a boat? The anticipation of an outlet for her creativity fired her enthusiasm. She had to make Grayson see her point. She just had to! She'd see her father's dream to fulfillment. She'd show those people who'd ridiculed him that he'd simply had insights well ahead of his time.

When she attempted to row, the oars spun clumsily in her hand, her efforts going for naught. "Of course, they need to be up and down." Aurora adjusted the paddles so they would cut cleanly through the water. "Much better. Nothing but common sense really, much like life."

Unbidden, an image flashed before her, a product of her ever-ready imagination. Grayson seated across from her, plying the paddles, while she leaned back decorously, trailing her fingers in languid relaxation through the water. His feet would be splayed apart, braced against the bottom of the boat, his long, strong legs revealed in form-fitting breeches. His sleeves would be rolled partway up his tanned, strong forearms. Beneath the dusting of dark hair, she saw the sinewy pull of muscles as he rowed. His shirt would be partly unbuttoned, she decided, affording her tantalizing glimpses of sweat-sheened muscles, heightened by the sunny day and his exertions.

She could smell his male, musky scent, as heady an aphrodisiac as the man himself. She saw herself slowly edge forward, kneel before him, playfully unfasten his trousers . . .

She blinked herself back to reality. Where on earth had those lascivious thoughts come from? While the sex act might be a pleasant diversion, it was hardly the way to bring Grayson around to her way of thinking. Levelheaded logic was what was required. Mutual cooperation and respect.

"Besides," she said aloud as she endeavored to steer a relatively straight course, "haven't you learned that no man is about to come along and make things easy?" Her father's death had been a shock; her hasty marriage a grave disappointment.

Grayson Thorne was the proverbial puzzle, the way he'd

caught her off guard in the summerhouse last night, and again in the library this morning. Clearly he enjoyed keeping people off guard. Luckily, she'd managed to match his moves with a few of her own, and he'd find that she was more to reckon with than she appeared. She'd simply wait for the right opportunity, then move him around to her way of thinking so subtly, he wouldn't even realize what was happening. The Gaslight would be everything she and her father had talked of, and more.

As Aurora renewed her determination to do her father's memory proud she glanced toward the gazebo, which for some strange reason did not seem to be getting any closer with her efforts.

It would be divine to laze about, to while away the lovely June afternoon in its secluded tranquillity. She could also rehearse her presentation in the privacy of the gazebo.

As she was attempting to maneuver the rowboat one of the oars slipped from her hand, unlocked, and plunked over the side into the water.

"Oh, dear!"

When Aurora stood and tried to reach for it, the boat see-sawed precariously. She scrambled for balance, found it, then caught her foot in a bailing can on the bottom of the boat and fell overboard.

Aurora thrashed wildly and somehow managed to flail to the boat, where she clung determinedly to its side as she tried to kick her feet. Her wet skirt wrapped about her legs, making movement next to impossible. The saturated long skirt also impeded her attempts to clamber back into the boat.

Holding fast to the boat with one hand, she struggled with the buttons fastening her skirt. As she fought her way free she felt the garment sink like a stone; she was grateful not to have suffered the same fate.

Gray could hardly credit his eyes. He'd arrived at the pond's edge in time to see Aurora stand upright in the boat and pitch headfirst into the water. Why was he even surprised? The woman was a walking disaster, tromping about where even an angel would exercise caution. And there was not one single angelic thing about her at this moment.

"Bloody hell!" He skinned out of his jacket and boots and hit the water in a running dive, reaching the boat and his waterlogged guest in short order.

"Good afternoon," she said, as if splashing about in daywear, clinging to an empty boat, was a normal pastime. "I can't quite seem to get back aboard."

"Do you swim?" Gray inquired.

"I'm afraid it's not something I've had the opportunity to learn, no."

He stood and scooped her up in his arms.

"Lucky for you, this pond was man-made and is not very deep."

"You mean I could have stood and walked to shore?"

"Well, it would have been slow going, but you only would have drowned if you had panicked."

"I never panic," Aurora said haughtily.

He carried Aurora the short distance to the gazebo and set her on her feet inside the structure. Then he returned for the boat, which he tied securely to the railing of the gazebo.

Aurora managed to look somewhat chastised in her bedraggled, skirtless state. Water poured from her blouse and knickers to puddle at her feet as she plunked herself upon the wooden bench and pulled off her sodden shoes and stockings.

Her hat was long gone. Her hair wreathed her head in soaking curls while her wet clothing stuck to her skin, leaving nothing to the imagination. Her breasts were high and taut, her nipples rigid from the cold. Her pantalettes clung to her legs and derriere, outlining her very pleasing shape.

"I suggest you get out of your wet things before you catch a chill," he remarked as he peeled off his shirt, wrung it out, and laid it over the gazebo railing. "They won't take long to dry in the sun. Fancy a glass of champagne while we wait?"

"A glass of champagne? Are you a magician?"

"Simply a good host." As Gray spoke, he opened a rustic built-in sideboard and pulled out a bottle of champagne in a silver bucket.

Aurora moved to his side, noting the condensation on the side of the chilled bottle. As she observed the deft way he opened the bottle and filled a glass for each of them, her eyes narrowed with suspicion. "How does there come to be chilled champagne in a gazebo in the middle of a pond?"

Grayson shrugged. "I believe in anticipating my guests' every whim. The servants were here early this morning, setting this up." He pulled out a compact wicker basket and delved inside. "Feel peckish?"

"Why don't we just go back to the house, so I can make myself decent?"

"Too much hustling about over there, in preparation for

tonight's party. We can talk here uninterrupted. You did wish an audience with me, did you not?"

"Not in my underpinnings. No."

"Not even when they're most fetching underpinnings?"

He was in his glory, Aurora knew, once more feeling totally in control and believing he held the upper hand—which she would continue to let him think.

"You're a very challenging man to try and figure out, Grayson Thorne."

"Nonsense," he said. "Men are simple creatures." He cut a piece of cheese as he spoke, speared it with the tip of the knife, and passed it her way. "It's women who are damnably complicated."

Aurora shook her head at the cheese. Her wet things were hideously clammy and uncomfortable. Reminding herself that she was a modern woman, eminently capable of taking care of herself, she shrugged free of her blouse and tossed it to Grayson, who caught it one-handed. "You've bigger hands than me. Mind wringing this out?"

She'd clearly surprised him, both by her actions and her words. The knowledge brought her a warm rush of satisfaction. Perhaps it wasn't only satisfaction? Perhaps it was Grayson, shirtless and even more appealing than her fanciful imaginings of him. In her daydream, his trousers hadn't been soaked, clinging to his legs with loving form, leaving absolutely nothing to the imagination. She felt herself grow warm at the direction of her thoughts. They were alone once more.

He watched her, as if somehow he knew she had undressed

for him. Brazen she might be, but not brazen enough to strip to her skin.

"I don't expect your guests will be overly scandalized when I creep upstairs in my knickers?"

"They have their own antics; I doubt they'll even notice. This lot tends to be fairly self-involved."

"Yet you're hosting them." Aurora reached past him and tore a chunk of bread from the baguette. "Am I permitted to guess why?"

He cut another chunk of cheese and Aurora accepted this one with a brief nod of thanks, enjoying herself. It was a mild, sunny day. An isolated setting. Stimulating male company. Champagne. Yes, this was a divine adventure, with the best yet to come as she got what she came for. Everything she'd set her sights on and more, she thought, recalling with a delicious thrill last evening's interlude in the summerhouse.

"You think I have ulterior motives for my party?"

"I know you have ulterior motives."

"And those motives would be?"

"It has something to do with your father's demise. Suspicious circumstances surrounding his death, perhaps? And you believe someone involved in the club holds the key."

"Don't!" His voice was unexpectedly sharp.

She'd been half-joking, making up the scenario as she went along. Clearly, her musings had hit close to the mark.

"Don't what?"

"Don't speak of this to anyone."

"Don't worry, I shan't."

"More to the point, don't attempt to pigeonhole me. For it's a game you won't win."

"Who says it's a game?" She swayed toward him as she spoke. He could smell the damp, sun-warmed tendrils of her hair, the hint of champagne on her breath, the musky woman-smell of her skin. It was a dangerous combination, even for him, who was quite adept at holding himself in check.

"You like to push people," Gray said thoughtfully.

"Sometimes. You seem to enjoy the chance to push back."

"What happens if I don't push you back?" He touched her as he spoke, finding the soft curve where shoulder meets neck. He saw her pulse jump at his touch and beat wildly in the hollow of her throat.

"You push and you pull in the most distracting of ways." Her voice was husky, but she wasn't backing away from his touch or his challenge.

On the contrary, she laid one hand against the wall of his chest, where it fluttered against his skin like the softest of butterfly wings. He liked the way she touched him. But appreciating a woman's touch could prove dangerous—or it could simply serve as an enjoyable diversion.

He opted for the second and pulled her toward him slowly. He could feel the warmth of her skin through the damp of her underclothes. "You think distracting you is what I'm all about?"

"I think distracting me is one thing you're definitely all about. A clumsy attempt to dissuade me from the reason that I'm here."

"Very well, then. I refuse to be true to form." He released

her and sat back, sprawled along the built-in wooden bench. "Make your pitch. Tell me what you want from me regarding the theater and why I ought to agree."

Gray had to hand it to her; she wasn't flustered by the spontaneity of their audience or the unorthodox setting. And she had done her research, he discovered as she drew a breath and began to speak.

"Historically speaking, people have always looked to be entertained. Since the beginning of time there have been troubadours, belly dancers, stage plays, and opera. You and I both know the theater; we know that mounting a play is risky and time-consuming. Actors, rehearsals, musicians, critics. And what if it's a flop? The moving picture is far less complicated. A screen and projector with someone to operate it are all that is required. The same piece of film strip is played over and over for different customers."

She stood before him, fueled by passion for her subject. While passion could be a good thing, it could also prove dangerous, for any intense emotion clouded a person's better judgment. In matters of the heart, as well as matters of business.

"Clearly, you see a future in moving pictures. What if you're mistaken?"

"I'm not. In the four years since the cinematograph was invented, pictures continue to be improved. Look at the progress from daguerreotype to Kodak."

"I admit, moving pictures are an interesting novelty at the moment. What of the novelty wearing off?"

Aurora could hear her father's voice as clearly as if he stood in the gazebo next to her. "The film pieces themselves are only bound to get more sophisticated. Already there is talk of marrying sound to the action, not unlike the wax cylinders they're using for phonographs. 'Tis the way of the future."

"You're a passionate little thing, aren't you?"

Aurora felt the intensity of his gaze as he leaned toward her, and she moistened her lips with the tip of her tongue. "If there's something I'm fixed on, I believe in pursuing it with everything I have."

"Right now there's something *I'm* fixed on," Gray said. "I find myself quite fixed on the lush, plump redness of your lips. And how they must taste. Soft and warm and quite, quite delectable."

"You're changing the subject."

"Or I'm just now reaching the subject that interests me, having been tantalized by your wet clothing for many minutes now."

"I didn't need rescuing from the water, you know. I would have managed fine on my own."

"But you were fun to rescue," Gray said. "And look where your impulsiveness led you. An impromptu picnic."

"This gazebo reminds me of the summerhouse at the far edge of the garden. Were they built at the same time?"

"They were," Gray said. "Same master craftsman. Very good with his hands." As he spoke, his fingers edged beneath the strap of her chemise and stroked her bare skin. "You have unbelievably soft skin."

Aurora couldn't move; his touch was a brand she craved. "What happens next with your guests?"

"A dance. More revelry and secret trysts. Couplings. Exchange of partners."

"Is that the part you look forward to? The exchange of partners?"

Was it her imagination, or did he stiffen slightly? "Unlike many of my contemporaries, I don't believe the grass is always greener elsewhere. I believe that with the right partner, one can truly achieve physical bliss."

"You're a romantic, then? A one-woman man, perhaps?"

"Romance? I'm talking about sexual appetite. And, like most men, I admit to the enjoyment of seeking out the one special woman who can truly satisfy me above a smorgasbord of partners."

"What is she like, this one woman for you?"

"I'm not sure," Grayson said. "Perhaps she has copper hair. And a taste for adventure."

Aurora pushed away his hand and jumped to her feet. "You're toying with me."

Grayson threw back his head in laughter. "Of course I am—you're devilish fun to tease. You take everything so seriously."

"Perhaps life is one endless game to you. But to me it's always been a serious proposition."

"Sit down, Aurora. Have some more champagne. In truth, I find your company most refreshing."

Refreshing? 'Twas almost insulting. For once, her confidence deserted her. Perhaps it had not been he in the summerhouse last evening, after all? Perhaps she had dallied with one of his guests and simply imagined it to be he. Her and her cursed imagination, painting the man as Grayson because she wished it so. How embarrassing if that were true; if the touch of a total stranger could lift her to such heights of passion.

Passion such as she might never know again. It seemed unfair to have to spend the rest of her days with only that one memory to sustain her.

"What is it?" he asked. "What did I say wrong?"

"I do not wish you to find me refreshing," she said haughtily.

"How would you have me think of you, then?"

What was it about this man? Usually her forthrightness had men backing down, stammering in chagrin. Not Grayson Thorne.

She could hardly admit she wished to hear that he fancied her, was captivated by her—dreamed longingly of a repeat of last eve's enchanted encounter.

"I would have you consider what I said about the Gaslight Theater and moving pictures. Don't destroy that beautiful old building."

"How else would you have me consider you?"

How could he possibly know there was more on her mind than moving pictures? "That will do nicely for now."

He caught her wrist and held it loosely, with just enough pressure to let her know he had her. His thumb stroked the soft inside of her wrist. "I know a bluff when I hear one. I suggest you not try your hand at poker." He continued to stroke her skin with long, slow, sensual strokes. "See how your pulse quickens at my touch."

"I'll have you know I'm good with games of chance."

"This game you play with me could well be the biggest chance you've ever gambled on."

"Anything big is worth the gamble."

"Even if you lose?"

"I don't play to lose."

"Perhaps, in this instance, there is something we both stand to win."

"Exactly! With your theater and my business plan, we really can't lose."

"Hang the business plan. I'm talking about us. Now. A summer solstice like no other. A fantasy where each and every desire is thoroughly sated." His voice lowered as his touch grew more bold. "I long to possess you. Your satin-smooth skin." Knuckles grazed the lace edging her chemise and seared the skin peeping overtop. "Your lush and delicious lips. I desire to lick and taste each and every one of your charming freckles." As he spoke, he lowered his lips to her shoulder and forged a warm, wet, hungry pathway to her collarbone. Aurora caught her breath, scarcely daring to breathe lest she break the spell. A faint breeze blew across the pond and ruffled her damp curls, its cool caress a contrast to Grayson's heated breath and hotter gaze.

"You wish me to be your paramour for the duration of my stay."

"Only if that is also what you wish."

"And if I refuse?"

"I will arrange for your return to the city. You have only to say the word."

"My prospects to lease or buy your theater—do they rest on my decision?"

Grayson swore and jumped to his feet. "What kind of man do you take me for?"

"One accustomed to getting his own way—in every regard."

"I don't allow personal feelings to interfere with business decisions."

"Good." Aurora rose. "Neither do I. But I must ask you one thing. Why me?"

Grayson appeared amused by her question.

"I warn you, I won't accept simple lust for a response. There are women here who are younger, more beautiful, and far more experienced and talented than I. Any of them, I'm quite certain, would be more than happy to give their host a tumble."

"The actresses, I fear, are interchangeable. You, Mrs. Tremblay, are unique."

"You fancy me because I am different?"

"I fancy you because you are you. Frustrating, fascinating, impulsive. You are many more things besides, but dull is not one."

"And you, sir, are most challenging as well." She waved one arm in a half circle. "On the surface you appear as transparent as the waters that surround us. Clear and simple, yet impossible to see into, no hint to their depths, and full of surprises."

"And you, my dear, are like the clouds overhead. Fleeting in appearance, impossible to hold."

"A cloud sounds far less joyful than water or sun."

"Your life, I sense, has been far from joyful."

How did he know her so well on such short acquaintance? Or had they both waited forever for this moment in time? This moment of truth?

A sense of rightness, of belonging she had never expected to feel, guided her steps as Aurora walked into his arms and twined her arms about his neck. "Fill me with joy. Show me everything I have missed."

"The sensory pleasures, I am happy to show you. The joy, you must discover for yourself."

"Do the two not go together?"

"Perhaps they can follow. One from without and one from within."

"Enough talk," Aurora said, raising her mouth to his.

"Agreed." Grayson lifted her up. He kicked their discarded clothing into a nest on the wood floor, and laid her gently atop them.

"Not very elegant makeshift digs, I fear, but 'twill have to do." He kissed her long and hard and deep.

Aurora sighed and held his head near hers when he would have withdrawn. "More!"

"Kissing you is divine. Like feeling something stir and come to life beneath me."

"I come fully to life because of you." Aurora shifted, urging him closer atop her. Her breasts chafed against her chemise, longing for the feel of his skin on hers. He freed her breasts from their confining undergarment and laved them with his tongue, starting a current of sensation Aurora felt in every part of her body. She arched her back, wanting, needing more. More of him against more of her. He plowed his hands through her hair and held her fast while his pelvis fitted itself to hers, matching the contours of her body.

"Fill me," Aurora entreated, undulating against him, delighted and amazed at the way they fit together as two pieces of an interlocking puzzle. A key in a lock.

"I intend to do just that," Grayson said. "But first I intend to tease you to distraction."

Chapter Five

Tease her to distraction? More like remove her totally into another sphere, one where responses and feelings were like nothing she had ever dared dream of.

Yet somehow, hadn't she always known such a place existed? Always believed, like Sleeping Beauty in the fairy tale, that one day the prince would come along and wake her with a kiss? Grayson's first kiss had stirred her to life in ways she had been incapable of imagining.

Last night in the summerhouse might seem like a dream, a part she'd been born to play to no audience save herself and her partner, but today was another matter.

Today was bathed in sunshine, awash in the very real sensation of Grayson's body pressed against hers in the most intimate of ways. No masks. No shadows. No phantoms. His gaze upon hers made no secret of whose touch had the power to send her to heights previously unknown.

Lazily he reached past her, plucked a piece of ice from the champagne bucket, and popped it in his mouth. As she watched, fascinated, those lips lowered, swooped, and locked on hers.

A jolt raced through her, hot and cold in tandem with the burning heat of his lips and the shocking cold of the ice. Delighted, enchanted, she passed the ice back and forth until it was melted to nothing; only to be immediately replaced by another.

In Grayson's talented fingers, the ice became an instrument of extreme stimulation. He rubbed it across her breasts and nipples, then blew on them. Hot. Cold. Hot again. Aurora squirmed. Her legs felt too heavy to move, yet the throbbing need at their juncture wouldn't allow her to remain still as he guided the ice lower. It slid across her ribs and abdomen to ring her navel, before he dipped it lower still, beneath the band edging her knickers to glide toward her hottest core.

Aurora held her breath as fiery fingers and frozen ice teamed together inside of her, the melting ice water underscored by her own slick spill of moisture.

"You're so hot," Grayson said, his fingers teasing her to distraction as promised. "You melted that ice in seconds."

Aurora arched her torso and raised herself against him.

Wantonly, her breasts brushed his chest. She felt them chafe in the most distracting of ways before she gave a frustrated tug at his trousers, desperate to feel all of him locked against all of her.

"I quite agree," Grayson said. "We're both wearing entirely too many garments."

He tugged her to her feet and knelt before her as he peeled away her pantalettes and buried his face against her stomach, licking, nipping, adoring her.

She twined her fingers through Grayson's hair as he lowered his dark head between her milk white thighs. Ripples of pleasure radiated to the tips of her toes and fingers, and she sobbed in need. How could he affect her so? Her body clamored for more as he licked his lips in satisfaction and slowly reclaimed his feet, taking her with him. As she felt him touch her everywhere, his hands like branding irons igniting her skin, it still wasn't enough. She needed him in her, on her, surrounding her.

"Kneel here for me."

How could she deny him anything? As she knelt on the bench and held fast to the railing before her, she heard him rummage in the picnic basket. What now?

"Sweets for the sweet." She glanced over her shoulder in time to see Grayson dip his hands into the pot of honey. Then he spread the sticky sweetness between her legs, anointing her. She quivered at his touch, at the sensation of the honey mixing with her own sweet juices. Aflame, she burned and chafed, wanting, needing more.

"Patience my lovely." Grayson positioned himself between

her legs and proceeded to feast. "Honey to and from your honey pot. An irresistible combination."

He lingered over the sensitive skin at the top of her thighs, licking the crease, front to back, that separated leg from buttocks. Aurora gritted her teeth and tightened her hold on the railing as she swayed with him and against him, adding her own rhythm to their dance.

As his tongue maneuvered its way deep inside, Aurora screamed. She tried to muffle the sound against her bare arm, to no avail.

"Delightful," he murmured against her, full of her. "Do that again."

Frantically she bucked and gyrated against him, his darting tongue, his questing lips. This time, when she came, the sound of her release echoed across the pond and reverberated through her.

"Very nice." Grayson resurfaced and skinned off his britches. "Now ask me again."

Aurora drank in the sight of the swollen hugeness of his cock, and her insides tingled anew in anticipation. "I want you. I need you."

"You're empty for me."

"Empty forever."

Grayson lay back on their makeshift bed. "Your turn to fill me."

Rather than position herself immediately atop him, Aurora knelt by his feet and paused in anticipation. With maddening slowness, she rubbed her sensitized breasts along his hair-roughened legs and over his hips. Reaching his middle, she circled his attentive, ramrod-stiff cock; grazed her nipples along its length, and heard him groan in response.

Upward she quested, exploring the hollow planes of his stomach. The hair was softer there, arrowing down his chest to ring his navel. She touched her lips to the softness. Such a contrast. Soft-furred skin. Hard, pulsing cock.

"Aurora." Impatiently he took hold of her, dragged her the rest of the way, and thrust himself inside of her. "Ride me."

Her hands grazed his chest, then settled alongside his shoulders for balance as she drew herself upright atop him. When she rose up, then plunged down, he groaned his approval. The sense of power, the knowledge that she pleasured him as he delighted her, drove her to new heights of ecstasy.

She bent forward and adjusted the angle of their bodies, only to feel anew the friction of his cock as it slid against her clit.

"Ohhhhh." Never had she known such freedom. She moved, unashamedly seeking to intensify her own sensory experience. First she leaned forward, then pivoted back and forth along his length till, sitting straight, she rode him up and down, controlling the speed at which he entered her. Slowly at first, she gradually sped up, experimenting with it all.

"You like that?"

"Yes," she said, as she swiveled side to side. "I like that as well, though. What do you like best?" She drew circles with her pelvis.

He grasped her hips and held her motionless, able to feel

his swollen length throbbing inside her. Playfully, she tightened her muscles and squeezed him with all her might. He gritted his teeth. She attempted to repeat her side-to-side swivel.

"Don't. I pray you. Or it's all over."

"Surely not so soon," she said.

"Surely not." He rolled over and took her with him. She stared up at him as he moved above her, loving the way the muscles bunched in his arms and shoulders. She stroked him, tentatively at first, then with growing intensity as he smiled his approval.

"I take it you like controlling the pace."

"What's wrong with the woman having the control for once?"

"Nothing. Except it could prove a mite embarrassing for the man." His rhythm inside her was steady and slow as he pulled all the way out, then buried himself inside of her as Aurora bent her knees to accommodate him deeper.

"Need more?" He pulled her legs up to rest on his shoulders.

"Yes!"

"I'm not coming until you do again."

"That's fine by me." Raising her hips, she angled her clit against his hardness.

"Touch us both," he said.

Aurora slid her hand between their slick, joined bodies and slowly spread her fingers to ring his cock and touch her clit. Elated, she felt their spilled juices, their mingled moisture, the incredible force of their joining. As she stroked, Grayson gradually increased the rhythmical pace at which he entered her, all the while watching her. Waiting.

He didn't wait long. The heat, the power, the intensity built and banked until it finally exploded. Her body bucked beneath his, her back arched, and she screamed as she came. He pumped harder. She screamed again as he plunged deeper still. Frenzied force carried them as, with a deep groan, he reached his own release, then eased down atop her, totally spent.

She felt the frantic gallop of his heart against hers, the way his breath fanned her face and stirred her hair as their breathing gradually slowed to normal. She ran her fingers along the length of his spine and felt his involuntary jerk of reaction. She smiled to herself, pleased that her touch could still stir him, and her fingers wriggled lower to cup his backside, rewarded by his heartfelt sigh of pleasure. She traced his backbone again and again. Above her, his body finally was still.

"My goodness." Aurora smoothed his shoulders, toyed with the tangle of his hair. "I do believe you outdid yourself."

"I'm quite afraid so. It's all a downward slide from here." He rolled to his side and tugged her with him, tucking her along his length. Cradled alongside him, she thrilled to the steady rise and fall of his breath in tandem with hers.

"Is it always that intense?" she inquired.

"Never," Grayson said.

"That's a shame," Aurora murmured. "Perhaps it just requires more practice."

"Perhaps it simply requires the right partner to practice with."

Would she ever have a partner more right for her than Grayson? She glanced upward to blue, sun-drenched skies, deliberately keeping the moment light. "Perhaps it's a result of being out of doors. The invigoration of fresh air."

"Not to mention the possibility of someone coming upon us," Grayson offered, with a lascivious chuckle.

"My goodness—I never thought of that." Aurora half sat and rummaged for something to shield her nakedness.

"Relax," he said. "We have the only boat. There's no possibility of anyone witnessing our being together."

"You're sure?"

"Absolutely."

"And we don't have to go back unless we want to? We could stay here forever if we chose?" She heard the wistfulness in her own words and tried to laugh it off. "But then I'd miss out on the next grand adventure, wouldn't I?" As she spoke she ran her hand along the flat of his abdomen. Not for the world would she have missed out on this adventure.

"There are always unexpected surprises ahead," Grayson said. "Come, let's get you washed up."

She pulled back. "I've been in once already, and it's cold."

He gave her a cocky look. "You've not yet been in with me to keep you warm."

"And just how do you propose to do that?"

"I'm quite sure something will come to me."

"What if I were to confess to a lifelong desire to bathe in the all-together."

"If we had more time, I'd teach you to swim."

"I'm not sure I'd be an apt pupil." She followed him down

the steps and into waist-high water. Water droplets on his shoulders and chest shone in the sunshine like flawless diamonds on the sun-bronzed perfection of his skin.

She started when he scooped up a handful of sand from the pond's bottom and gently rubbed her with it. "What are you doing?"

"It's better than soap, the way it polishes the skin. Not that yours needs it. Yours already shines like a pearl, and feels like satin."

"I love the sensation. It's very . . . stimulating." She turned and presented her back in order to feel the grainy caress across her shoulders, down her spine, past her waist to her buttocks. Grayson abruptly pulled her toward him, and she was surprised to feel him stir against her backside.

"Isn't the water too cold for you to be aroused?"

"Apparently not," he said. "Equally apparent is the fact that you excite me like no other woman has in a very long time."

She thrilled to his words, reached up to clasp his head in her hands and nuzzle herself against him. She inhaled the scent of their damp, naked flesh as she enjoyed the way his hardened muscles abutted her rounded curves. She rubbed against him, arousing him from semihard to fully erect.

He leaned forward, nipped at her earlobe, and cooled the sun-warmed skin of her neck. "I have an idea."

Aurora shimmied against him. "Another good idea?"

"I'm sure you'll agree."

In back of the gazebo, a large boulder rose out of the water. Aurora allowed him to position her facing the rock, hands braced on its sun-warmed surface, and sighed aloud when his tongue and lips traced the ridge of her spine from neck to buttocks as his cock found its way to the delightfully round contours of her behind.

He reached between her legs, rubbed her inner lips, and heard her sharply indrawn breath. She was still hot and wet from earlier, and he eased himself into the velvet sweetness of her. As he reached around and touched her nipples, he felt them spring to attention in instantaneous response. Fresh wet warmth was followed by her throaty moan of pleasure, and he continued to nibble her neck as he palmed her nipples and pumped inside her.

"Touch yourself," he said. "Rub your clit and intensify your pleasure."

"I'm not certain I can handle more pleasure," she murmured.

"I dare you to try."

"I never could resist a dare."

Once again she surprised him with her inventiveness and enthusiasm. Not only did she touch herself, she also gently thumbed his balls and the base of his cock. Somehow she managed to find that incredibly sensitive patch of skin between his balls and his anus, and when her thumb brushed him there he tensed, fighting for control.

"I said touch yourself," he said from between gritted teeth.

"Eventually. Right now I'm having far too much fun touching you."

Her responsiveness made him crazy and he flat-palmed her nipples, feeling their budded hardness. She felt so incredible. All of her. Rounded derriere. Pale limbs. Vulnerable neck. He nibbled that sweet spot as he slipped a hand between her legs, touching her in the same free fashion she touched him.

Her breath caught as he shifted slightly, altered the angle of penetration, and varied the pace. He mimicked her earlier swiveling motion, staying deep, filling her, driving her as wild as she drove him.

She was so hot. So wet. So tight, it was all he could do to breathe. To concentrate. To catch her rhythm as her orgasm built, and match his pace to hers. He timed it to perfection so that when her muscles started to spasm, to tighten around his primed cock and signal the beginning of the end, he was more than ready. He heard her delighted cry seconds before he felt himself explode inside of her, awash in the juices of their pleasure.

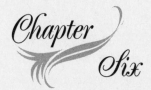

Chapter Six

When Aurora returned to her room to find a bath waiting, along with a forest green cloak and mask artfully fanned across her bed, she couldn't still a ripple of anticipation for the evening's adventure ahead.

The festivities appeared to be in full swing by the time she had refreshed herself with a bath, a nap, and the tray of food delivered to her door. Was Grayson seeing to her needs? Or were all guests treated so? Several hours had passed, and already she was eager to see him again, to be partnered with him in this bizarre solstice party.

Dance music blared from the ballroom, and she followed

the toe-tapping rhythm of "Hot Time in the Old Town." The guests were clearly ready for a hot time. Particularly those focused on their own, far more intimate dance, cavorting on the stairs and in the hallway. She tried hard not to stare, aware of the way she and Grayson had found their own special rhythm earlier.

Where was Grayson? Why was no matching forest green mate awaiting her appearance downstairs? She felt conspicuously alone as she stepped past a burgundy-garbed couple locked in an embrace, who she doubted were even aware of her presence.

The main floor of the mansion was lit by flickering wall sconces and elaborate candelabra that added an eerie sense of unreality to the gathering, reminding her of a stage set.

The entire weekend had the air of a play within a play. Even Aurora, no stranger to the world of theater, was having a devil of a time sifting reality from make-believe. It was disquieting. For even though nothing seemed quite real, some of it had to be. Did anyone else make the distinction? She sidled past two women in feathered masks and headpieces as they kissed and embraced, ogled by two men wearing their colors.

As she paused in the doorway of the ballroom, Aurora was jostled by a drunken couple in bright purple who pushed by in a cloud of alcohol fumes. The room she stood poised to step into was a restless sea of gyrating colors and frantic energy. Nowhere in the den of iniquity did she see a lone green-cloaked man, eagerly awaiting her appearance.

Aurora accepted a glass of champagne from a passing

waiter and observed the Rose and Thorn Club in all its secretive splendor. Carte blanche promiscuity, tarted up under guise of creative license. A brilliant concept, really.

A man in a harlequin costume waved a wand and released a shimmer of rainbow-hued bubbles through the crowd. Guests applauded and raised their hands in an effort to catch the elusive beauties, which slowly melted to air, one by one. Elusive as her absent host.

"Dance?"

Aurora spun about, face-to-face with broad masculine shoulders clad in forest green. Dark eyes blinked at her from behind the mask.

"It's about time. I was beginning to think you had abandoned me." She stepped closer, then stopped. Wrong eyes. "You're not Grayson."

"Somehow, I didn't expect you'd be fooled for long. Gray has been delayed. He sent me in his stead."

She frowned. "Beau?"

The man before her laughed. "Hardly. I'm Randall Ames, Gray's right-hand man and overall minion. Although he tells people I'm his secretary, we're actually very good friends."

"Then I suggest that you carry a message to your good friend." Aurora tapped the man's cloaked chest for emphasis. "Tell him I am not some interchangeable puppet like his other guests, to be passed about to the highest bidder."

"Aurora, that wasn't his intent. Gray didn't want you to be left on your own. He'll be along as soon as he can."

"And in the meantime?"

"In the meantime, I'm not a half-bad dancer and conversationalist."

"I'm more than capable of taking care of myself."

"This crowd is a little unpredictable."

"And Grayson isn't?"

The man before her laughed, a masculine hoot of genuine amusement. "Well put. I can see why Gray's intrigued."

"Intrigued. Is that his word?"

"Very much so, beginning with your unorthodox arrival."

"If it's all the same to you, I'll pass on your generous offer and amuse myself watching the others."

"As you wish. But do remember, things are never quite as they seem."

Aurora nodded in agreement. "Starting with Mr. Thorne himself."

"Gray has a lot to contend with these days."

"These days as opposed to others?"

"You're right, of course. He takes his responsibilities most seriously."

"I don't care to be thought of as one of his responsibilities."

"I'll be sure to tell him that."

Aurora stepped through the open French doors into the formal courtyard, which was partly illuminated by flickering torches. She could hear the gurgle of a fountain nearby in the shadows.

She veered right, slid into her own shadowy crevice out of sight of anyone who might be watching, and took a deep breath. Pungent cigar smoke overrode the fragrance of the garden. A shadow shifted on the bench near the fountain and turned into a trysting couple. Did the owner of the cigar watch in secret? Or did he watch her? The thought was unsettling. Aurora shifted deeper into the shadows and settled on a stone bench from which she could observe without being seen.

From her vantage point, she glanced up at the moon. If not totally full this evening, it would be tomorrow night. She could see the cool, mysterious light, the marbled bluish features in its round face, and wondered why it never looked happy. Perhaps because the sun got more worship and adoration. Yet some cultures revered the moon more than the sun, paying homage to the fact that the Moon-mother gives her light at night when it is needed most, whereas the sun only shines during the day.

She was an interloper. Not part of the club. Nor any part of Grayson Thorne's world. Sleeping in Celeste Grayson's bed and pillaging the other woman's wardrobe seemed as wrong as the way, even now, she longed for Grayson. His presence. His kiss. His embrace.

He'd offered her an escape this afternoon, which she'd declined, intent on the physical pleasures she was discovering for the first time in her life. If she really yearned to be part of the festivities, she'd be mingling with the other guests, with or without Grayson on her arm.

Damn the man and his effective way of distracting her from the reason she'd shown up in the first place. She had no intention of accepting "no" in any form. He could lease her the theater, sell her the theater, or partner with her in the theater. But one way or another, the theater would prevail. Her show of moving pictures would go on.

"I apologize for the unavoidable delay. And the fact that you took exception to my sending Randall in my stead."

It took a minute to register that she hadn't imagined his presence, his words. That he was real, standing alongside her.

Aurora rose. She couldn't give Grayson the advantage of standing over her. "I'm not accustomed to feeling so out of place as I do among your guests."

"Come, come, Aurora. These women are your contemporaries. I'm certain you've shared the stage with some of them."

"I'm not ashamed of my past."

"Nor should you be."

"We weren't all born with the advantage of wealth."

"No. You, for instance, married it."

Aurora stiffened. How did he know so much about her? "I did not marry Hubert for his money."

"You also didn't marry him for his strength of character."

Aurora had no answer; Grayson spoke nothing but the truth.

"I, on the other hand, am well equipped to appreciate you in every way a man appreciates a fine woman. Wine or woman, I make it a point never to settle for less than the best."

"You amuse yourself at my expense."

"And here I thought the pleasure had been mutual."

It *had* been—and entirely too intense, much like her host. First she'd longed for his presence, now couldn't wait to escape.

"I'll leave you to your thoughts." Aurora took her leave

abruptly and soon got lost in the garden, the music growing faint in the distance. Where was she? Her new surroundings seemed more disorienting than the maze.

She lost all track of time as she wandered first one way, then another. Eventually the trees gave way to an open meadow that shimmered silver in the moonlight and dipped up a hillside into deep shadow. A faint breeze whispered through the rippling grasses. The moon backlit the impressive outline of a single broad-trunked tree that dominated the open space. Even the tree reminded her of Grayson, lord and master of all he oversaw. Not till she drew closer did she see the silhouette of a swing suspended from one sturdy bough. What whimsical, playful mind had wrought such a treat?

"Go ahead. It's safe enough."

She spun to face Grayson, silently close. "Do you never grow weary of following me?"

"I feel a certain responsibility for your safety."

"What gives you cause to think I would ever be safe in your presence?"

She heard him blow out a breath. "What makes you think I find safety in yours?"

Could it be she unsettled him as he unsettled her? "I believe your friend said you find me intriguing."

"Intriguing is only the beginning."

"If intrigued is the beginning, where might it end?"

"Who says it has to end?"

"All things end, Grayson. Life. Marriage. A tryst. A week's end out of time."

He took her hand. "Not here and not now, they don't. I believe we create our own destiny."

Go ahead, whispered her traitorous body. *You'll never get a chance again to experience anything like this.* She'd spent her life "doing" for everyone else. First, trying to make it up to her father because her mother died, then trying to be all things to Hubert that he wasn't capable of. Even the moving pictures, dedicated to her father's memory. *Just this once, be selfish. Put your own needs first.*

"I can't," she whispered. "I don't know how."

How about this, then? Grayson needs you more than you need him.

The truth hit with a jolt, leaving Aurora feeling as if a huge weight had been lifted from her back. This was something she could do, as long as she was needed. And watching Grayson in the moonlight, seeing the way he watched her, all hesitation vanished.

The moon was her only witness as she stepped into the circle of his embrace and tilted her face up, hungry for his kiss. As he drew her to him she felt him exhale unsteadily and knew she'd made the right choice. For he hadn't been at all sure of her. She felt the first waves of desire ripple through him and into her, and was struck anew by how well their bodies fit. The instant anticipation from her female parts wanted, needed, craved all he had to give. Would she ever tire of this man? Reach saturation?

Her skin tingled, her breasts begged for his touch, and her lips drank greedily from his, while she touched him as urgently as he touched her. He cupped her bottom, clasped her to him, and let her know that he wanted her with equal fervor.

"I forgot to explain to you about the cloaks."

"You said our colors would match."

"The other guests are naked beneath. Far more convenient."

"Are you naked beneath?"

"I will be in a trice."

Feeling bold and tossing all caution to the wind, Aurora followed Grayson's lead and discarded her clothing till all that remained were her mask and her cloak. She found the sensual swish of the heavy satin lining against her bare skin as erotic as the secret whisper of the breeze through the grass, heightening the way each individual grass blade tickled her legs while the breeze teased her bare skin.

"You do introduce me to new levels of daring, Mr. Thorne." She twirled about in gay abandon, heady in her newfound freedom.

"Lord help us all," Grayson said. "Climb aboard the swing with me. We'll head for the moon."

The moon smiled down upon them as Grayson settled her aboard. She sat on his lap facing him, her bare legs straddling his hips. As she gripped the ropes, her hands below his, she felt a renewed shiver of anticipation.

"All aboard. And we're off."

Beneath them, the ground seemed to disappear. Toward the heavens they swung, gathering speed as they sailed out over the moonlight-dappled field.

"Why do I feel anything is possible? Including reaching

the moon." Aurora could feel the heat from Grayson's skin warming hers. The moon-kissed night air added its magic caress as the swing's motion catapulted them higher and higher.

"Now that we've no clothing impeding us, I have another idea," Grayson murmured.

"I must confess, I'm growing to like your ideas," Aurora said.

"I feel confident you'll like this one best of all."

As he spoke, he reached down and stroked between her legs. Beneath his touch her body opened like a flower, allowed him access to her very soul.

"You're breathtaking in the moonlight. Your hair turns from red-gold to silver-bronze. Your eyes hide your secrets, even as they reveal your longings."

"What longings do you see?"

"The way you get so wet the second I touch you. Begging for me to make you come, yet challenging me to leave you quivering with need as I deny you final release. You want me lodged deep inside you. You long to experience the fullest possible possession. To feel me in the very deepest depths of your soul."

"Yes." How did he know? It seemed he had always known, better than she, exactly what she needed. Did he also suspect, as she did, that their total possession of each other would never be enough?

The two of them would always have new heights to scale, new challenges to master, and new adventures to set forth upon. Yet here and now there existed naught but the two of them. And it was everything. All she would ever need.

He grasped her hips and raised her up. Knowing she was safe forever in his arms, she released her hold on the swing and wrapped her arms around his torso. She drew warmth from his skin and strength from his person, along with an outpouring of fresh desire.

She could feel him, rock hard and hot, seeking her warmth. She wriggled slightly, slid herself along his length, dampening him with her liquid desire, and felt a surge of satisfaction as his hold on her tightened.

Their mouths greeted each other, licking, tasting, devouring each other in a fevered passion that stole her breath as she endeavored to draw closer, to invade his very soul as he had invaded hers.

"Stay still," he said, his voice raw with desire.

"How can I . . . oh," she said with a breathy sigh, as he sought and found his way inside her. Aurora caught her breath at the incredible friction resulting from their joining, in tandem with the swaying movement of the swing beneath them.

"Oh my word!" Waves of rapture lapped their way through her body, intensified by the heat. Their motion. The way the moonlight bathed them in a shimmer of unreality. It was too much! Too intense—this place where nothing was real, yet everything existed.

The swing.

The stars.

Her lover.

As she felt Grayson move inside her, become a part of her she never wanted to relinquish, she responded with an acceleration of her own, riding him into the next universe. She could feel his pulsing length gliding in and out in the same smooth motion as the swing. Her insides strained, reached to hold on even as she let go.

Then she shattered into a million shimmering pieces, each of which soared upward to lodge in the heavens, rendering her the brightest jewels in the sky. And left her mortal body spent and shaking in Grayson's arms as the swing slowed, easing them back into the real world.

"You took me with you," he said. "Wherever it was you went."

"To heaven and beyond," she murmured.

"Shall we see if we can surpass all that?"

Renewed desire built low in her belly and spread through her limbs. "Whatever you wish."

"I wish for nothing more than to pleasure you."

He punctuated his words with a slow, deep upward thrust that stole her breath. He held her legs and used her for leverage, kneading her thighs, the slightest brush of his skin a further enhancement to her mindless state of arousal. She raised her hips, moving first with him, then against him, then with him again. She felt him in every fiber of her being, embraced the way he filled her, completed her, in all the ways a woman longs to be touched by her lover, inside and out. Her breathing quickened. Her muscles clenched around his pulsing, thrusting length as together they created their own fever of ecstasy.

She'd been wrong, Aurora thought, staring up into the starlit universe. She'd thought their physical joining could never be enough. But as he filled her and she filled him, their hearts and souls embraced, along with their bodies.

If this was all a dream, it was one she never wanted to awaken from.

Chapter Seven

Aurora stirred, reluctant to return to the real world anytime soon. Swinging away her cares, her responsibilities, locked here in Grayson's arms . . .

She drew away slightly and gave herself a mental shake. Since when was she one to float along, to let some man take charge of her life? Just because Grayson was the in-control type and good at it didn't mean he should have control of her.

No doubt he was as tired of responsibility as she was. Witness this estate he was maintaining, the legion of servants he was in charge of, not to mention seeing to his brother while he kept the home fires burning for a gadabout actress mother in the bargain. Oh, yes. Aurora knew all about shouldering the burden of other people relying on one.

Gray felt her stirring and pulled her back against him, but in a supportive way. "Where are you off to so fast?"

"Hmmmmm." How nice to lean against his broad chest and pretend there was nothing else that mattered save the here and now. Too nice. Perhaps that was one reason she hadn't taken her leave when offered the opportunity earlier today. If this was a moment out of time, she wanted to wring out every last drop she could.

"I must confess," she said. "When I climbed aboard that hot-air balloon yesterday and we went off, I harbored secret longings just to keep going, never to go back. I have similar urges right now—just to stay like this, removed from the daily bothers."

"You have a lot of daily bothers?"

"No more than most, I'd wager. Doubtless fewer than you."

"What makes you say that?"

"Well, I've met your younger brother. I'm aware of your mother's reputation. I've spoken with your friend Randall, and seen firsthand the size and scope of your estate. Which just happens to be overrun by the notorious Rose and Thorn Club, at the moment."

"I must confess, I'm not feeling too bothered by any of it right now. I'm totally enraptured by my companion."

"Still, the bothers are lurking out there—like some fire-eating dragon one must set off to slay."

"You've slain your share, I take it?"

"My mother died when I was ten. My father never quite got over it."

"So he put down his sword, and you picked it up, heavy as it was for a child."

She nodded. Tears prickled the back of her eyes as she swallowed the egg-sized lump in her throat. "He was ahead of his time in so many ways, and he suffered a lot of ridicule as he struggled to invent a new type of camera. One that would capture motion, not just stills."

"Did he invent the cinematograph?"

"Sadly, no. His melancholy and frustration got the best of him. But I want to show moving pictures and honor his memory, his dreams."

"Why my theater?"

"It's too beautiful to be torn down. It deserves a second life." She didn't tell him her more personal reasons: how the theater symbolized a time when all was right in her world, her mother and father and herself together there onstage. If the theater were torn down, she felt her dreams would go along with it.

"I give you my word, by the close of the weekend, I shall have my answers, and you'll have yours."

Aurora knew he spoke of something far more important to him than simply the future of a building he had recently inherited.

The swing slowed to a bare shudder and stopped. Grayson slid to his feet, Aurora still wrapped about him, and carried her to where they had discarded their clothing. Why did it seem like a lifetime ago?

"You needn't return to the party if you don't care to."

"Am I being sent to my room like a child?"

"I'm starting to suspect that neither you nor I had much chance to act childishly. Even when we were children."

His words were far too close to the truth. How had Grayson, on such short acquaintance, learned things about her that no one else had ever guessed?

With Grayson in the lead, their return to the mansion was easily accomplished, the moonlight their only illumination.

"The party does seem to be quite ribald," Aurora murmured, as they reached the formal courtyard garden. Torchlight played upon a naked couple who cavorted in the fountain, screaming and splashing in gay abandon amidst a waterfall of froth and bubbles, clearly unperturbed by their audience. "How are the bubbles formed?" she asked. "I saw some earlier. They were like magic."

"A little elixir my housekeeper discovered one washday. I knew this would be the crowd to appreciate them."

"Indeed."

"There you are, Gray. I've been looking everywhere for you."

How did the newcomer recognize Grayson? Aurora wondered. Certainly he was taller than most men, but his height was not enough of a distinguishing feature.

"What now, Randall?"

Aurora relaxed. Of course. Randall would know what color his friend sported, having been the stand-in earlier.

"It's Julian. He's quite drunk, quite belligerent. Claims someone has absconded with his 'date.' "

"Let me guess—that someone being Beau, no doubt."

"Everyone else seems happily partnered up. Julian is quite miffed."

"Where is he now?"

"I've taken the liberty of locking him in your study with a bottle of brandy, before he upset the others."

"I'll go see if I can placate him." He turned to Aurora. "Can I trust you to stay out of mischief in my absence?"

She bristled. "I don't go seeking trouble. It manages to find me."

"Keep an eye on her, would you, Randall?"

Aurora stuck out her tongue at Grayson's retreating back, then clapped a hand to her mouth, realizing how childish her action was. She turned to Randall, hoping he hadn't seen. "I met Beau earlier, but who's Julian?"

"Julian, along with Gray's father, helped found the club. He's also Gray's godfather."

"You've known the family a long time, I take it."

"I've known Gray since our school years. My own father frittered away the family money. When Gray inherited all this, he needed someone he could trust to be a part of it."

"I take it he doesn't trust too many people."

"He's cautious by nature."

"Tell me, does he ever take off his mask?"

"The masks are part of the Rose and Thorn."

"That's not the mask to which I was referring. He gives away very little. And observes a lot."

"The Thornes and the Graysons have their skeletons, like any other family. You'll have to find out what you want to know from Gray."

"I wasn't being nosy."

"You're curious. Can't say as I blame you; they're a curious lot. 'Specially this crew, this weekend."

Aurora smoothed the edges of her satin mask. "People act differently when they feel safely anonymous."

"We all have something to hide. After all, nakedness is revealing. It makes us vulnerable."

"No one can accuse Gray of being vulnerable."

"No. But between you and me, I think it would do him a world of good to shatter that iron control of his."

"Grayson's strength is an integral part of who he is."

"Yet nothing comes without a price tag, does it?"

And the cost to Grayson for being strong, staying strong—was it the same that it cost her, or different? She changed the subject. "You offered to partner me on the dance floor earlier. Is the offer still open?"

"My pleasure." He crooked his arm toward her a tad too rakishly for Aurora's tastes. Or perhaps she was just comparing him to Grayson. No doubt from this time forward she'd compare every man she met to Grayson; all were destined to come up short.

"You didn't boast in vain about your prowess on the dance floor," Aurora said, as Randall twirled her expertly among the other couples.

"It's a skill I've not had much opportunity to practice lately."

"Why is that?"

"No beautiful woman to encourage me."

"You're flirting with me."

"You're right. May I confess to enjoying it? I don't believe I have indulged in idle flirtation before."

"You and Grayson both treat life too seriously. Flirting is a gift you bestow upon another."

"I never thought of it like that before."

She smiled. "I could offer you new perspective on a great number of things."

"Including monopolizing my partner, I do believe."

They both froze in midstep at Grayson's sudden reappearance.

"That was fast work," Randall said, as he turned Aurora back over to their host.

"So was yours," Grayson said dryly.

"Julian is all right now?"

" 'Twas easily remedied."

"Good job. Anything interesting come to the fore?"

Aurora watched the look exchanged between the two men and knew their conversation was very pointed yet deliberately vague.

"Not yet. But the weekend is far from over."

What *was* Grayson hoping to learn this weekend?

"Too true." Randall bowed toward Aurora. "I enjoyed our opportunity to dance. And to flirt."

With his words, the tension evaporated. Aurora stepped into Grayson's arms as if she belonged there. She pulled his head close to hers and spoke in a voice no one else could hear over the music. To any onlookers, they were simply locked in an intimate version of the dance.

"Let me help," she said.

"Help with what? Sober up my drunken godfather?"

"I'm hardly stupid, Grayson. I know what this weekend is all about. And how I can be of use to you."

"Really." He pulled back, his eyes unreadable behind his mask.

"I'm stubborn, you know. You're best off accepting my offer. Otherwise, I'll just blunder about and possibly make matters worse."

"Your words sound suspiciously like blackmail."

"Someone here this weekend holds the key to your father's death. I can help you learn what happened."

"You are quite mistaken, in your melodramatic way."

"What are you afraid of?"

His shoulders and spine stiffened, and she could feel the mental distance he placed between them. "You speak of fear. I have none."

"We all have fears. Is yours honesty?"

"Aurora, you overstep your bounds."

"I know no bounds. And neither do you, for you read me as you read that book of Braille earlier. You possess a perfect grasp for some passages, while others remain a total mystery."

"Fanciful."

"There is so much we share, and honesty is integral. I am with you solely because I choose to be. No masked phantom. No mystery lover. You, and you alone, are my companion for the duration of my stay. I want to know *you,* not simply whomever you choose to reveal behind the mask at this moment. I know your father's death is eating at you and that someone here has a key to unlock the answers about his death.

No one knows who I am. Look at the advantage that affords me."

"Stay out of it. All of it. I have no need of your help, and no desire to be examined on the head of a pin."

Aurora smiled to herself as Grayson released her abruptly, then turned and stalked away. Bolted, really, at the candor of her speech. She watched him retreat, knowing he'd be back. His strength wouldn't allow him to flee in the face of adversity.

Left to her own devices, Aurora wandered into the dining room, where the long polished table nearly buckled beneath scores of sumptuous dishes. She wouldn't have thought Mrs. Blossom would take to preparing the array of foods spread before her, all lush and sensual, and clearly intended to be eaten with the fingers. Oysters. Stuffed figs. Rich tartlets and savory pastry rolls. Tiny erotic sweets and cakes.

As she circled the table, she paused to help herself to a sweet. Abruptly the hair on the back of her neck began to prickle with the unmistakable feeling of being observed. She spun about. The verandah door stood open, the space beyond deep in shadow. As the breeze filtered past, she caught the faint yet familiar scent of cigar smoke she had smelled earlier.

Why would someone be watching her? All the men here had their pick from the bevy of beauties, three full days and nights to sample whomever they wished.

"Aurora. Aurora, is that you?"

She looked up, and a mask obscured the features but not

the luminous smile greeting her from across the table. "Misty. How did you know?"

"No one else has that same flamboyant hair. How did you know it was me?"

"I'd recognize your smile anywhere. Besides, I recall hearing a while back that you'd become involved with the Rose and Thorn."

"I have been for a while now. I had no idea you'd joined in. Isn't it something?"

"It's very new to me," Aurora said cautiously.

"Well, it should do wonders for your career. It has for mine."

"I'm counting on that."

"Did you happen to meet our host yet?"

"As a matter of fact, I have."

"Isn't he divine?" Misty fluttered her eyelashes and clutched her bosom dramatically.

"I thought he seemed a little aloof, actually."

"That's half the charm. Once those aloof ones come to heel, they're the best."

"There you are, my dear," said a male voice. "I've quite been missing you."

"Sorry, Julian. I ran into an old friend."

"So I see. I pray, do introduce us. For by the end of the party, we'll all be much more intimately acquainted."

"Aurora Tremblay, meet Julian Fields. One of the founders of the club, and a true patron of the theater."

"A pleasure," Aurora murmured, finding her hand engulfed in both of his a trifle too tightly. There was something unsettling about the eyes perusing her from behind his mask. Or perhaps it was just due to the mask itself, obscuring his other features.

"I have a feeling the pleasure has not yet been met," he murmured smoothly, raising her hand to his lips. As his moist lips grazed the skin on the back of her hand, Aurora resisted the urge to snatch her hand back. Like Misty, Julian wore scarlet, which meant Misty had been the one who had disappeared for a while earlier, upsetting her partner. Wasn't that an interesting turn of events?

"I adore this estate," Misty said. "So many hidden nooks and crannies to explore. I fear three nights won't prove near long enough."

Julian clapped a possessive hand on Misty's bottom and gave Aurora a lecherous wink. "Which reminds me, there's a certain little cranny of yours I have a yen to explore, my dear. Shall we?" He punctuated his words with a crude laugh.

Misty nodded, but her lack of enthusiasm didn't escape Aurora's notice. "Good to see you, Aurora."

"And you."

Back in the ballroom, the formality of matching cloaks with partners seemed to have loosened to a drunken free-for-all. No one seemed to be paying much attention to who climbed aboard whom, the evening having become one huge orgy.

Was Grayson taking his ease with one of the many willing females here? Did they all view him as divine?

Feeling very much on her own again, Aurora managed to locate Hudson, Grayson's butler. He seemed as dismayed by the proceedings as she was and only too happy to fulfill her request for hot water for a bath.

The sounds of the revelry followed her up the stairs and into Celeste's room before it faded from earshot. It had been quite the full day, she thought as she submerged herself in the water's steamy heat. From her library flirtation with Grayson, to her mishap in the pond and gazebo picnic; all before tonight's party, the meadow sojourn, and the ride aboard the swing. More adventures in one day than she could have ever dreamed.

But the adventure was far from over. For even though Grayson had disdained her offer of help, she was determined to assist him one way or the other. She knew firsthand how it felt to lose a parent in questionable circumstances. The rumors and whispers and inferences made peace difficult to obtain.

The water's divine warmth seeped through her, easing tender twinges in muscles never before used. Squeezing the flannel, she sent a ticklish trail of warm water across her shoulder and neck. She closed her eyes and imagined it was the rasp of Grayson's delectable tongue stimulating her sensitive nerve endings. Her entire body tensed, as if with anticipation. She was becoming truly insatiable for the man.

Would he seek her out tonight? Or had he had his fill of her? She tipped her head back. He consumed her thoughts, which in turn intensified her longings. The more times they coupled, the more she longed to be one with him, in every meaning of the word. Her nipples tingled as she recalled the excitement of his kiss. The way his lips shaped and reshaped the contours of her breasts, suckling her.

She cupped her breasts in the cradle of her palms and found their weight satisfying. She hoped Grayson had, as well. They were neither overly large or small, with nipples the most delicate pink hue, the palest blush against the alabaster of her skin. She'd always hated her freckles, but no longer. Not after the way Grayson had kissed and delighted over each and every one of them, sparking their beauty.

Her nipples tightened, and she grazed them with her thumbs, rewarded by a pleasant warmth flooding through her and a pull from deep within.

Shameless.

Wanton.

Delightful.

A woman's body was truly a marvel, especially when she had the opportunity to share it with a man she found to be her equal.

Her husband had been far too weak for the likes of her. Far more interested in cards and drink and that nasty white powder he indulged in with his friends, which made him even weaker and less effectual.

How fortunate she was to discover the sensual delights shared between a woman and man. A truly erotic adventure. If today was all she had, it would have to serve for a lifetime—yet selfishly, she longed for more.

She trailed her fingers through the water, down between her legs. Her body was tireless, ready once more to receive Grayson and the pleasure he afforded her.

When she felt something impossibly soft brush her cheek,

she opened her eyes to see a shower of effervescent bubbles raining down upon her. Grayson stood over her.

"You looked so peaceful, I didn't want to disturb you."

Aurora straightened and reached upward to capture one of the fleeting beauties. It evaded her grasp, ashimmer in the candlelight. "I confess to having had the most lascivious thoughts of you."

"Really."

Grayson sent a fresh shower of bubbles her way. One landed atop her breast, as light and loving a caress as his lips.

"I was angry with you earlier," he said.

"I won't apologize for my frank speech."

He bent over her, his arms resting on either side of the tub. "I didn't come here seeking an apology."

She couldn't resist touching his bare hand, feeling the strength that was such an integral part of him. "Then why?"

"I couldn't stay away." He sounded as if the confession was torn from him.

"Good," Aurora said with satisfaction, touching him more freely. "I was longing for you. I don't want you to stay away."

"I thought if I had you once, it would take away the craving."

"Last night in the summerhouse," Aurora said.

"The summerhouse," he agreed. "I tried to maintain my anonymity, but you refused to let me get away with it."

"Why should I allow you to 'get away' with a thing?"

"You allow me this." He caressed her breast, and she sighed at the pleasure wrought by his touch. "You encourage me to touch you in all manner of ways."

"I like it when you touch me."

"I want to do more than simply touch. I need possession."

"Possession? I choose to share myself with you; that is something entirely different," Aurora said.

"Lie back," Grayson said. "I'll wash your hair."

"Like a lady's maid?" Aurora asked with amusement.

"Why not?" He moved toward her, rolling his sleeves up to reveal the corded strength in his arms. Aurora slid back down in the tub and bowed her back so her hair was submerged; the graceful movement raised her breasts toward him.

Gray caught his breath at the sensuous grace of her body; like a water nymph or a mermaid offering her breasts proudly to him like the most precious of gifts. Just as she had offered herself to him for the next two days. And much as he wished he could walk away, he knew he could not.

Perhaps he was more his mother's son than he wanted to believe. For hadn't that been her claim, that men desired her, and she couldn't say no? Aurora wanted him, and he was equally powerless to say no, even as he hated himself for it.

No one had ever gotten under his skin the way Aurora had. From the second she hopped nimbly out of that balloon, she'd been flinging him one challenge after another until his head was fairly reeling. And even though he'd vowed to stay away, here he was, back at her side like some lovesick swain.

He'd left her on the dance floor earlier and regretted his actions immediately, for while he might deny the pull she exerted over him, there was no denying her appeal. She intrigued him in a way that no one else did. The gift of her laughter. Her inner strength. Her stubborn independence. Her delightfully sensuous body and its powerful response to his touch.

He raked his hands through the wet strands of her hair, feeling it twine around his fingers and wrist as effectively as Aurora herself had twined around something inside him. Something he'd long thought untouchable. Unreachable.

He used his magic bubble elixir to suds her hair while she sat straight and proud for his ministrations. Beautiful. Enthralling. Enchanting. His for two more days, and nights.

"No one has washed my hair since I was a very young child."

Gray caressed the damp strands and let them drift through his fingers. "It's alive with a fire all its own. You should see it in the candlelight—burning with fire, the way you do. Alive from the inside out."

As he spoke, he made a cup of his hands and rinsed the suds from her hair. Then he tugged her gently to her feet, encased her in a huge, soft towel, and proceeded to dry her off, starting with her satiny shoulders and arms. Her pert breasts. The womanly curve of her hips and waist and behind. The long, fine shape of her wondrous legs. The delicate, elegant feet.

Her skin glowed pink from the warmth of her bath as she stood before him, fragrant and delectable. Had he ever wanted a woman more?

"Lie before the fire for me."

"Whatever for?"

"So I may admire the sheen of your skin in the firelight. And it will help to dry your hair."

A thick rug lay before the fire, as if awaiting Aurora's arrival. Seeming completely comfortable in her nudity, she took a seat before the flames, displayed herself in an artful pose, and arranged the strands of her hair across her shoulders and back like a fiery cloak. She plucked a strand and frowned at it.

"You really like the color of my hair?"

"I adore the color of your hair," Gray said. He adored everything about her in this instant.

"Did you bring me champagne?"

"Of course." He fetched her a glass.

She nodded her thanks and took a sip, then licked the rim. He watched and envied the glass rim the caress of her lips and tongue. Madness. He was a man possessed, bewitched.

"Shouldn't you be attending to the needs of your other guests?"

"There is only one guest whose needs I desire to attend to this evening."

"Grayson, Grayson." She narrowed her gaze playfully at him. "What ever will I do with you?"

"Whatever you wish, I fear."

"Tie you up? Ravage you?"

His loins quickened at the thought, although he kept his voice casual. "If you think that would please you."

"I rather enjoy the idea of rendering you helpless."

"You have managed that feat without the use of bonds, my dear. Besides, if you were to restrain me, I'd be unable to use my hands to pleasure you."

"That's true," Aurora said. "But I might enjoy the act of subtle torture by teasing."

Gray swallowed with difficulty; even his breath felt tight. The woman was truly amazing. He was accustomed to partners who required coaxing, who submitted to his persuasive charms while feigning reluctance, then expressed remorsefulness afterward. 'Twas part of the ritual he'd come to expect but never particularly enjoyed. With Aurora, things were different. She was his equal, as willing and enthusiastic a partner as he was.

"Without even trying, you manage to tease. Look at your breasts, how they beg for my touch."

"You flatter yourself. Any touch will do." Aurora selected a section of nearly dry hair and feathered its silky tips across her rosy-hued nipples. Gray watched the way they puckered in response. She cupped one in her hand, blew on it, then teased it with the tips of her hair.

"Fickle, are they not?"

Gray rose abruptly. "Fickle as most women, I suppose." Yet as fickle as Aurora might prove to be, he couldn't stop wanting her.

She rolled onto her stomach, pillowed her cheek across one arm, and peeked enchantingly up at him. "Not all women are fickle."

"You were married. Were you true to him?"

He watched her face cloud.

It was as he thought; no woman was capable of fidelity. Most were simply more discreet than Celeste.

"My husband, as you stated earlier, was a weak man. And

he was far more interested in pursuits other than me. We were never one in the true sense." Aurora rolled onto her back and held her arms out to him. "Make love to me, Grayson. Here before the fire."

"Tell me what you need me to do."

"I need you to be my lover."

"Be more specific."

"I need you to kiss me. I die for want of your kiss."

"To kiss you how?"

"To kiss me everywhere."

"What of my pleasure?"

"You may enjoy it, also." She gave him a seductive smile. "Even now, your breathing quickens. Your member hardens and strains against the front of your trousers. You desire nothing more than to mount me, to take your ease between my thighs. Yet you remain fully clothed, pretending indifference." She rose to all fours and made her way toward him, an exaggerated sway to her hips. "I know you're not indifferent to me, Grayson, much as you pretend otherwise." Using him for leverage, she pulled herself up the length of his body, making sure she rubbed herself against him in all the most vulnerable places.

"You think you're so clever." He raked his fingers through her hair, then used his hold to pull her head back, to bare her throat for his kiss.

"You're wearing far too many clothes. I'm guessing it makes you feel somehow still in control."

"Don't you feel vulnerable in your nakedness?"

"Quite the contrary. I know what the sight of me does to you. I feel empowered."

"You're impossibly beautiful," he said, the words sounding guttural with the depth of his longing. "The firelight kisses your skin, turns your hair to molten flame." He wanted her so badly he ached, yet he was determined to master his desires.

"Still you keep your distance." She danced away as she spoke. "For what are you waiting? For me to seduce you?"

He was already thoroughly seduced, caught up in a desire so fierce it frightened him, for it pushed all other thoughts from his mind. He was a man who prided himself on not giving in to his baser desires, for stalwartly maintaining control—a control Aurora was hell-bent on shaking.

"Have it your way," she said, flouncing away from him. She seated herself before the dressing table and selected a jar of scented cream from the dozens available. She removed the lid and took a sniff. "Lovely."

She turned to face him, dipped her fingers into the jar, and scooped a measure of the cream, then slowly, sensually, applied the concoction to her skin. White-on-white. Which was more pure? He watched, mesmerized by the sight of her lithe, pale arms, the way she smoothed the cream across her shoulders and chest.

Next she turned her attention to her feet. Gray sucked in his breath as she raised first one graceful leg, then the other, all the while massaging cream into her limbs with a slow and sensuous stroke. When she widened her legs, exposing her womanly core, he thought he might explode at the sight of her rubbing cream the length of her thighs, across her stomach, and up to her breasts.

Gray could scarcely breathe, couldn't rip his eyes from

the sight before him. She'd once made her living onstage; was this, even now, an act? Did she perform solely for his enjoyment? For it seemed that she spent an inordinate amount of time smoothing the cream onto her breasts. Surely she must enjoy the feel of her own touch, for he heard her tiny sigh of pleasure. He noted the way she took her time caressing her breasts and her nipples, and watched her thighs go slack as her lids grew heavy with renewed desire.

His cock screamed at him to rip off his clothes, to tumble her then and there. But he stood as if frozen.

"Grayson," she purred. As she spoke, she used the middle finger of each hand, finger bent, to caress each nipple in ever-widening circles.

Teasingly she trailed her finger down the flat plane of her stomach to her navel, circled her navel, then skittered lower, into that love nest of feminine secrets. With her other hand she lifted her hair up and away from her back and her shoulders.

"Be a love and rub cream on my back for me, would you?"

How could he resist? He moved as if sleepwalking, his eyes never leaving the wellspring of her femininity, the way she lightly touched herself.

He dipped his fingers into the jar of thick, rich cream. As he smoothed it across her back and shoulders, he resisted the urge to kiss each and every delightful freckle. She arched her back into him the way a kitten would. He could just make out the way her fingers disappeared into the golden red triangle between her legs, dipping in and out, moist from her own juices. He could smell the scent of her desire, and his mouth watered with the urge to sample her, to show her pleasure she had never dared imagine.

He held himself in check with the greatest difficulty—till she rose and bent over the stool, offering him the pert cheeks of her ass.

"Don't forget my bottom," she said.

How could he possibly forget its round lushness? The way the globes of her backside sleeked into the length of her legs. With a groan of surrender he dropped to his knees behind her, cupped the lush fullness in his hands, then buried his face in her welcoming warmth. Reverently he rubbed his cheeks against its satiny softness and inhaled her warm, clean fragrance. Then, slowly, he began to lick.

He began with the crease at the top of her thighs, slowly working his way around nearly to her hipbone, where he paused to sample the indentation of her waist, before finding her spine. Then he cupped both cheeks in his hands and nibbled his way up her back. He was starving, and she was food. He was parched, and she was an oasis. When he reached her shoulders, he allowed his tongue to glide back down as if her spine was one giant slide, sending him between the rounded cheeks to that vulnerable tiny rosebud of her anus.

He felt her tense as his tongue made contact. He liked that he could startle her. Treat her to sensations new and different. And she tasted delicious. He slid his hands around to where she'd been touching herself earlier and inserted two fingers into the wet, welcome warmth of her as his tongue continued to lave her from behind, seeking out each and every one of her secrets. Slowly, deliberately, he increased the pace, tonguing her while his fingers were inside her, till he felt her internal muscles tense and clench around his fingers. She was so wet.

"Think you can tease and torture *me,* do you?"

Chapter Eight

Her moan of pleasure made him smile.

"No contest. You win this round," she sighed.

"And yet I've barely begun."

He felt the responsive way her muscles quivered against him, inside and out. Exquisite!

He swung her around to sit atop the stool, so he could apply his attention to her beautiful legs. To anoint the inside skin of her silken thighs, and relish the entranceway to that delicious inner woman. He frowned at the sight of faint red traces, a legacy of their first coupling. Lightly, reverently he nipped at her, careful not to mark further the perfection of her skin as he slowly found his way to that steaming inner core.

The catch in her breathing told him she was close. He thrilled to the way she panted with exertion as she strained toward a completion only he could provide. Still he lingered, fascinated by a tiny, velvetlike mole near the top of one leg.

"Grayson." She clutched his hair and tugged, urged him to where she needed him most.

She was so hot, so wet, shaking with need. Finally, he delved toward those delicious inner lips. As he parted their sleek folds, he discovered the pulsating force of that tiny nubbin, which he delicately grazed with his tongue.

It was Aurora's turn to surprise him, for as she arched and shrieked her pleasure, a squirt of warm liquid hit his tongue.

Gray reared back, stunned. He'd heard of such a thing happening on rare occasions. Never before had he actually experienced the wonderment of it. Fascinated, he absorbed the aftershocks that rippled through her as he continued to lave and lick and savor and taste, wondering if it might happen again.

Would he never get enough of her? Like a man gorging himself on his favorite meal, he continued to indulge himself with the taste and texture and delight of her. Beneath his ministrations he felt her inner tension begin to rebuild. Everything shuddered and tightened as she started that journey back to the summit. But rather than compliantly allowing him his own way, she reached for him and unfastened his pants.

"I want you so badly." Her voice shook almost as much as

her hands as she urged his engorged tip toward that hot, wet, delectable center.

He drew back to meet her gaze. "Am I not pleasing you?"

She watched him, heavy-lidded with desire. "It would please me more to feel you inside of me."

"Brazen, aren't you?"

"The whole of me is aflame," she said as she unbuttoned his shirt and buried her nose against his chest.

"Allow me, then, to quench those flames."

"No one but you." Aurora rose and led the way to the makeshift bed before the fire. Gray stepped from his pants and followed, amused by the way she took the lead.

She stroked him briefly, admiring his form, then guided him to her entranceway. As Gray took his ease in the embrace of her hips, she rose up to greet him with her welcome warmth. Abruptly he stopped as the pleasure, the overwhelming intensity, proved almost more than he could bear. He'd yet to lose control, and wasn't about to start now.

She lifted her head, eyes staring intensely into his. "Why did you stop?"

"I want it to last as long as possible," he said, knowing as he spoke that the two remaining days she belonged to him would never be enough.

"You're in control," she said happily.

If only that were the case, Gray thought, as her hands touched him everywhere, branding him hers. He felt her nails abrade his shoulders. Her knuckles grazed his chest, before her fingertips found and tweaked his nipples, then gently tugged the hair on his chest. She sighed, clearly loving the sensation of touch. He tensed as she pulled him to her, clasping his ass in an effort to increase the pressure and pace of their joining.

"I thought it was my turn to be in control."

"Only if it suits."

"And does this suit?"

"Oh, it suits."

As he moved slowly, rhythmically in and out of her, the age-old dance of woman to man, he felt the quickening of her muscles. His body embraced the way her pleasure spiraled into small ripples of delight, each one battering him with more intensity, inviting him to join her in the ultimate release. An urge he fought with everything he had.

If only he could stay like this forever, her gloving him like warm, wet velvet. So hot. So responsive to his every move. He thrust in deep and stayed there, offering only slight, subtle nudges of him against her. She trembled beneath him, urged him deeper still, then reached up and helped herself to his kiss.

Her undulation started with a slow sweep of her tongue in his mouth, a sweep he swore he could feel all the way to his cock. As he swallowed her screams of pleasure, he let them carry him with her, until he could hold off no longer. And when she pulsed and sobbed and shattered into what felt like a million starbursts, he responded with a mind-numbing ejaculation that seemed to go on forever.

They held each other close and took their time as they drifted back to reality. "How does that happen?" Aurora whispered from where she lay cradled next to him.

"Well, my member fits snugly into your—"

"I know how *that* happens. I mean, how does it . . . Just when I think it can't possibly be more, suddenly it is."

"Consider it a special gift from the gods."

"I like that," Aurora said as she moved more snugly against him.

"Explain to me why we're on this hard floor rather than your soft bed," Gray said.

"A new experience," Aurora replied. "I wanted to see the firelight play against your skin."

He pressed a kiss upon her brow. "That's my line to you. Can't you come up with something more original?"

"More original than you? Hardly."

"I've been called many things over the years; original has never been one of them."

Aurora shrugged. "Other people obviously don't see you in the same light as I do."

"I'd wager that to be true."

"Now," she said. "Time to lay some plans for the morrow."

"What scheme have you afoot? A new adventure for a new day?"

"My friend Misty is here, and believes I'm one of the actresses. It ought to be relatively easy for me to infiltrate their group and see what I can find out about the night your father died. Someone knows something."

She felt his disapproval in the way he stiffened against her. "Leave it alone, Aurora. It's my concern."

"You do what you need to do, Grayson. But having me approach it from the other side will give you a decided advantage."

"I shall send you away if you insist upon continuing in this vein."

She shook her head. "To think I took you to be a man who goes after what he wants."

"My means are my own."

"Fine." Aurora rolled away from him. "Have it your own way."

"I don't want you interfering."

"I never interfere. Now if you don't mind, I'm rather sleepy. It's been a full day."

"It's nearly dawn—and none of this lot will be stirring till well after noon, I wager."

"Perfect." Aurora pulled on a wrap and stepped out onto her verandah. Dawn of a new day: the perfect opportunity to begin putting her plan into action.

Grayson joined her on the verandah. "Very well, then. If you insist, we'll use you for bait."

Her guard rose instantly. Grayson wasn't the sort given to a sudden change of heart.

"I could certainly be bait," she said cautiously.

"There were signs of a struggle the day my father died," Grayson said. "A piece of the Rose and Thorn emblem broke off a member's ring."

"So find who wears the damaged ring, and you find the killer."

"I doubt it's quite that simple."

"Nothing ever is." She waved an expansive hand to the east horizon. "Take the sunrise, for example. Ought not that be simple? The sun pops up. The sky lightens and heralds the start of a new day. But we both know it's far more complex than that."

"As complicated as a woman, perhaps?"

She laughed. "We are a secret society, you know."

"That I will believe."

"Magnificent, is it not?" Aurora asked reverently. For from a tiny slip of light sprang fire; intense burning color, magnificence and raw power in its most primitive form. Molten gold turned orange, pink, and red, backlighting a primary blue sky. "Mother Nature has a very subtle way of making me feel small and insignificant." She turned to him, touched him in a way that branded his core as the sun branded the sky. "We draw our power from nature." Her words rang with such passion, such belief.

"Have you always believed that anything is possible?"

"My life has always been a mixture of make-believe and reality. What else could I possibly believe in, other than endless possibilities?" She turned her attention from the dawn to the matter at hand. "Do the Rose and Thorn members all wear their rings?"

"They're supposed to. But I can hardly demand a close-up inspection of each ring."

She lightly traced the outline of his hand. "You're not wearing yours."

"No. And I won't."

"Not ever?"

"As my father's heir, I inherited my entrée to the club. It's not an avenue I ever would have pursued on my own."

"Can you decline?"

"Most assuredly. Once I unmask the man responsible for my father's death, I'll have no further use for the group."

"And together we shall spark new life into the Gaslight Theater, with the coming of the moving pictures."

She wasn't doing any of this because she cared about him, Gray reminded himself; it was only because of that wretched theater. She'd never understand. The theater that obviously brought to mind happy days for Aurora represented much of what went wrong between his parents to him. Celeste's infamy and his father's ill-fated partnership with Julian to name just a few. Gray had vowed years ago to go it alone, in business as well as his personal life. However, for the time being, if Aurora believed she was of some use to him and his cause, it would keep her occupied and out of his way.

Though he didn't want to have her out of his bed. *Never allow a woman to distract you from your goals,* he reminded himself.

He turned abruptly to face her. "I'll leave you to seek some sleep now. You'll need all your energies for the party tonight."

"Will you sleep, also?" she asked softly.

With you beside me. He bit back the automatic response. "I don't have a need for much sleep," he said shortly.

She took a step closer, as if seeing already the distance he was trying so hard to insert between them. "Lucky you," she said. "Will you stay while I drift off?"

"Another time, perhaps. There are things requiring my attention."

"Those responsibilities of which we spoke earlier?"

"Exactly." For a moment he felt himself weaken, and strengthened his resolve. "Sleep well, my dear."

AURORA DREAMED OF FOG. Thick and hazy and disorienting, it muffled her senses of sight and sound. She ought to have felt panicked, yet through it all, she knew Grayson would be there for her and that she had naught to fear.

Had she merely dreamed of the fog or had she conjured it up? Aurora wondered as she stumbled from bed, her head still fuzzy with irregular hours of sleep. She must have slept away the entire day, for dusk had stealthily entered the room and mysterious shadows lurked just beyond her peripheral vision, where all was a haze.

She went to the window, but the grounds were cloaked in shadow, ensnared in mysterious fingers of fog.

At the nightstand, as Aurora splashed cool water on her face she tried to recall her sunrise conversation with Grayson. It concerned the ring. She needed to learn which man wore the damaged ring. After debating what she ought to wear beneath her cloak tonight, she smiled once she was dressed, well pleased with her decision.

She wrapped herself in the claret-colored cloak she found draped across the foot of her bed, but her smile faded upon catching sight of the accompanying mask, fashioned like an executioner's hood. Would everyone's mask be of a similar design? The headpiece would effectively disguise her hair as well as her features, so no one would know who she was. Not even Grayson.

She pulled the mask over her head. It felt hot and confining, claustrophobic. Sound was muffled. Even her movements felt awkward and clumsy. She ripped the mask off and flung it aside, where it lay puddled on the bedcovering like a pool of red wine. Or blood. She shuddered at her fancifulness as she made herself ready.

Faint party sounds filtered upstairs as she spritzed on perfume and finally replaced her mask. Let the other actresses be naked beneath their cloaks; she favored her choice.

Once downstairs, anonymity again proved the order of the evening, and individual voices were difficult to distinguish with the hooded masks. Table games of chance with dice or cards occupied the attention of the guests, who all mingled freely, partaking from the glittering fountain of champagne in the center of the ballroom.

"Welcome." A masked man greeted her as she stepped inside the room. "Care to try your luck at the tables?"

"I believe I'll take a few minutes to get my bearings first."

"Remember, the auction takes place at midnight."

"The auction?"

"Tonight the men bid for the companion of their choice."

"But I thought . . . What of the colors?"

The man only laughed and drifted away as if she'd said something funny.

A woman dressed like a gypsy whirled past her. She muttered something that sounded like, "Beware the thorn," as she brushed by, leaving Aurora more confused than ever. In her wake passed a masked man who handed Aurora a long-stemmed red rose whose stem had been carefully shorn of thorns.

"A rose with no thorns," Aurora murmured. So if this wasn't the thorn she was to be careful of, what was?

Holding the rose, Aurora slowly wended her way through the crowded room, from gaming table to gaming table. Did Grayson know about the auction? Surely he knew which color she sported. Surely he wouldn't allow some other man to lay claim to her.

Her gaze circled the room. Her pulse raced as she realized all the men wore black tuxedos, their features obscured by identical hooded black masks. The costumes lent a sinister feel to the evening's activities.

"Rings," she murmured to herself as she fetched a glass of champagne. "Now is the perfect opportunity to study their rings." She tucked her rose down the front of her cloak and felt its stem ride against her breastbone.

She sidled up to a felt-covered gaming table, where a lone player faced the dealer. She felt the way he watched her from behind the eyeholes of his mask, unable to tell if it was friendly interest or threatening menace.

"Care to place a bet?" His words were distinguishable but not his voice.

Aurora shook her head. She watched closely as he captured the die. The sound of them knocking together in his cupped palms was almost like the rattle of bones. Light glinted off his ring. Intact. Aurora let out a deep, uneasy breath, aware she was starting to perspire. He won his toss.

She wandered to the next table, then the next, never quite able to shake the feeling that someone was charting her every movement.

Surely no one could know what she was about? When she felt herself tapped on the shoulder from behind, she jumped guiltily. Obviously, subterfuge was not her best talent.

It was one of the girls, who leaned in close and raised her voice to be heard. "It's almost time for the auction."

Aurora nodded vaguely. The problem with the men wearing identical tuxedos was that as they moved around, she had no way to distinguish one from the other. Although she'd seen dozens of rings, she could be viewing the same scant handful over and over.

Surely there was a better way to help Grayson. She glanced around the room. If only she knew for certain which one he was, they could confer in private. But she had no way of knowing which hooded figure he was, or even if he was in attendance. Surely he was here somewhere, waiting to bid on her at the auction.

A lone, dark figure stood off to one side near a curtained alcove, watching her. Come to think of it, he'd been watching her since she had first come downstairs. She knew it was the same man, for he wore no ring. It had to be Grayson.

Her relief was short-lived. It could also be his father's killer, choosing not to wear the damaged ring lest it give him away.

She leveled her gaze and stared back. Their eyes locked. Surely she'd know if her observer was indeed Grayson. Wouldn't she feel something? Shouldn't her blood sing, her pulse accelerate?

Ridiculous! They were too far apart for her inner senses to recognize Grayson, let alone respond to his presence.

The man made his way to the front of the room, where he

tapped his champagne glass with a spoon. Perhaps it *was* Grayson, being host. A hush fell over the crowd; the gaming tables fell silent.

"And now gentlemen of the Rose and Thorn, the event you have all been anticipating: the club's annual slave auction. Your chance to bid on the beauty of your choosing. The woman who will be your slave for the remainder of the evening.

"The challenge is that you have no idea which lovely is the rose of your choice. If I could have the ladies please line up here at the front of the room." There was an obedient shuffling as the women, including Aurora, did his bidding.

"Gentlemen, you may look but not touch. You know, of course, that each and every one is beautiful as well as infinitely talented. There is no thorn among these roses. But masked and cloaked, do you recognize the one who quickens your blood faster than her scintillating sisters?"

Damn this hooded mask! She could make out the words but not recognize the voice. As he spoke, one of the gaming dealers walked among the girls and Aurora heard a muffled clanking. Before she knew it, she was fastened to the women on either side of her, bound to both by a loose-linked chain on each wrist.

"What the . . . ?" Aurora tugged at hers but was unable to free herself.

"Don't worry, love," said the woman on her right. "The sight of the chains gets the gents right stirred up. Some of the sods really believe they're buying a slave."

"But . . ."

"It's all part of the pretense. Auction tonight, erotic stage play tomorrow. Gotta give the gents their money's worth." As she spoke she flashed a length of bare leg from beneath her persimmon cloak, much to the delight of the men milling about among the girls. Aurora squealed as someone rubbed up behind her and pinched her behind.

"Now, now, gentlemen. You know the rules. Look but don't touch."

"How do we know it's real if we don't grab a handful?"

"Buyer beware," intoned their host, with a lecherous laugh.

The buyer wasn't the only one to beware, Aurora thought as she eyed the sea of black-hooded masks swimming before her. What was she doing here?

Giving herself freely in passion to Grayson was one thing. But to find herself lined up like livestock, to be handed over to the highest bidder? How could she escape?

As the bidding began, Aurora tried not to panic.

Perhaps no one would post a bid for her. Surely the men knew which actresses held their fancy and had managed to ascertain their favorite's color during the course of the evening. Her hopes were dashed once the bidding got under way, for the men were lively, ribald, fiercely competitive; each winner jubilant, each loser clearly dashed.

They bid with tokens won during the gaming earlier, Aurora realized, not real money. So this was all part and parcel of their game, one they were well versed in from years past. The most successful gambler had his pick of women. And most men, she soon realized, didn't much care which woman they won, as long as they didn't repeatedly lose the bid—thus making the auction their biggest game of chance.

All too soon, it was her turn. She was instructed to take one step forward. The chains pulled tight as she did so. Blinking owlishly behind her mask, she scanned the crowd. Which was Grayson? Would he recognize her? More to the point, had he been successful at the gaming tables should the bidding grow intense? But perhaps no one would bother to bid on her at all.

Her hopes were short-lived. The bidding began briskly. As the price grew higher the men began to drop out until only two remained, one of whom was the man hosting the event. Up close, she saw he was too short to be Grayson, and her heart sank as she realized he'd been watching her all evening, determined to make her his.

His opponent, whom Aurora was unable to make out, stood at back of the crowd, so much in shadow that she was unable to discern if he was short or tall, stout or thin, while the mask muffled her hearing.

Grayson signaled his bid. The woman clearly had not a single lick of sense. He'd known the exact second Aurora entered the room. He'd watched her accept the thornless rose he passed her, observed the way she tucked it close to her heart, not knowing from whence it came.

He'd not had full knowledge of the auction, and by the time he tried to reach Aurora, to warn her to take her leave, it was too late. She'd been chained up amongst the other women, about to be claimed like chattel.

He knew very well who bid against him: Julian. He knew, also, that his godfather had been hankering after Aurora from the very first. Likely she was the one woman here whom Julian had yet to sample. Grayson had played hard at the gaming tables, winning often and winning big.

The question was, had he been luckier than Julian?

Chapter Nine

Beneath the wretched mask, Aurora tried in vain to moisten her dry lips. She didn't want to be here. She didn't belong, a fact made even more obvious when the other women began directing hostile glances her way once it grew obvious that neither man was about to back down in his quest to claim her.

"Silly buggers. Don't they know we're all the same in the dark?" voiced someone from behind her.

A second woman spoke up loud enough for all to hear. "What do you figure this one does that's so special?"

Aurora shifted her weight from foot to foot. Was it her imagination, or did the chains grow tighter as the bidding escalated? She began to wish with all her heart that she'd never ballooned onto Grayson's estate, never wound up in the midst of this midsummer madness.

But that would mean never having known Grayson.

She forced her attention back to the bidding war in time to hear the latest offer from the back of the room. Her gaze flew to the man near the front. Behind the mask his eyes gleamed with steely determination, and Aurora's breath snagged. He opened his mouth, then closed it abruptly. A waiting hush of anticipation befell those watching. The silence grew to deafening proportion.

When he spoke, his voice was coolly impartial. "Sold to the persistent gentleman in the rear of the room. Next."

Aurora let out her breath in a rush, sensing she was not yet done with the man at the front, who continued to watch her covertly as the bidding ensued, even as he successfully claimed one of the other actresses for himself.

At long last the auction was over, and each man received a tiny silver key to unlock his lady. Aurora glanced up at her champion, whose eyes gave away nothing. She rubbed her wrists as she heard the click of her freedom. Or was he simply releasing her to a different confinement?

When he crooked an arm her way, Aurora hesitated. Surely if Grayson stood before her, he'd give her some sign to set her mind at ease. He knew she was only in attendance to help him. Or did he? She watched him closely, waiting for a wink, some small gesture of reassurance, but none was forthcoming. Her heart was heavy as she tucked her hand through the crook of his elbow.

"Are we . . . Are we leaving the party so soon?"

"Surely you find yourself as anxious as I to be alone someplace private?"

She could find nothing familiar about his voice, and very little comfort in his words or the way he caught her close to his side. "Actually," Aurora said, "I fancy a breath of fresh air. Shall we take a short stroll through the grounds first?"

Perhaps outside, under cover of darkness, she could lose her companion and hood and escape to the safety of her room.

He pulled up abruptly and stood facing her. If not actually blocking her way, his stance indicated he was fully prepared to do so. "Perhaps it wasn't made clear earlier—you are my slave for the night."

Aurora took affront to his actions and his words. "I don't fancy being anyone's slave," she said coolly. "And I have a strong dislike for being ordered around."

His mouth thinned behind his mask. "Be warned: A good fight only serves to heighten the excitement. Now come."

Before she could anticipate his intentions he grasped the bottom edges of her mask and spun it around, blanketing her in darkness.

"I can't breathe!"

"Hold still." He flipped up the bottom of the mask, freeing her nose and mouth, while effectively doubling the covering over her eyes. She gulped in a welcome lungful of air.

"Why are you doing this? Where are you taking me?"

"Slave girls remain silent till granted permission to speak."

He kept firm hold of her as he escorted Aurora from the ballroom, down hallways, around corners, up and down stairs, till she was totally disoriented.

The sounds of the party receded in the distance till she could no longer hear it at all. All she heard was her own labored breathing. Or was it his?

Finally, he stopped. She heard the rasp of a key in a lock, the creak of a knob turning and a door opening before she was pushed inside a room. Then the ominous thud as the door closed, the key scraped. When Aurora raised her hands to her mask, he physically restrained her.

With his hands atop hers, she knew, and all but sagged against him with relief. Grayson's hands. Grayson's touch.

So what game did he play at? Testing her loyalty, perhaps? 'Twas a game two could play as easily as one.

"Am I to remain in the dark?"

"Do you not find your lack of vision sharpens the other senses?"

"At this moment, I feel the room's chill."

"That will never do. Stand here, and I'll light the fire."

Aurora moved the way he steered her, then gasped as her hands were roughly grasped, clasped around what had to be a bedpost, and efficiently lashed tight.

"There," he said in obvious satisfaction. "Now I needn't worry about any attempts on your part to bolt or rip off your mask."

She almost told him right then and there that she knew it was he, but a faint niggle of excitement stopped her.

He knew who she was . . . but not that she'd guessed his

identity. If he wanted to play slave and master, who was she to ruin their game?

So, what would get Grayson the most stirred up? Meek and compliant? Fearful and begging for release? She knew he'd have naught but scorn for any woman he perceived to be meek or afraid.

Someone who fought his advances? It would be difficult to fight him, when even now she craved his kiss, longed for his touch.

When she heard him return to her side, she pulled against her bonds. "Untie me, you bully. Let me look upon you and see what sort of man confines a helpless woman."

"I think not. The helpless part, I mean." He unfastened her cloak and it slipped to the ground near her feet. Undaunted, she kicked it aside.

"This is nice," he said approvingly, toying with the neckline of her frock. Aurora bit back her smile. She'd had Grayson in mind when she'd dressed for the upcoming evening. The frock was elegant in its simplicity; a sheer fall of body-hugging ivory silk identical in color to her skin, which rendered it difficult to ascertain where the frock ended and the woman began. The garment was no doubt intended to be worn only in the privacy of one's own room, for it dipped low in front and clung to her bosom and hips, emphasizing the fact that she wore not a stitch beneath.

She could well imagine how she must look, bound and masked, with the firelight silhouetting her naked limbs beneath the sheer gown. Grayson would be able to clearly discern her breasts, the outline of her nipples, rigid with excitement. The way her hips swept into the rounded curve of her bottom, and the outline of her legs.

She shifted slightly and felt the way silk prickled the soft curls guarding her Venus mound. She felt herself grow moist with anticipation. Provocatively, she circled her lips with her tongue, picturing them glistening wet in the firelight. Dark red. Begging for his kiss.

"What are you doing?" she asked.

"Looking at you."

"Anticipating what you're going to do with me?"

"Anticipation can indeed heighten the ultimate pleasure," he agreed.

"And will we experience pleasure?"

"I believe a pleasurable outcome is inevitable." He slid a hand across one breast, teased her nipple with his palm.

Her response was swift, startling them both as she shifted side to side, maximizing his touch and heightening her own enjoyment.

"You like that?"

"Untie me, and I'll show you just how much."

"Not yet." She felt hot, damp moisture as his mouth replaced his hand. Gently he suckled her through the fabric, rolling his tongue lazily around the nipple.

Aurora exhaled breathily, feeling the instant tug of pleasurable sensation from breast to womb.

"Still interested in putting up a fight?" he inquired lazily.

"You did tell me a good fight heightens the excitement, did you not?"

"Indeed. But I also told you you're my slave for the night. A slave is subservient. Obedient. Unquestioning."

"Perhaps you should return me for a different slave. One whom you would surely find more pleasing, with her meek nature."

"You have fire," he said. "Fire can be most useful."

"Fire can also destroy."

"Is that your desire? To destroy me?"

She had no wish to destroy him, but she would welcome the opportunity to bring him to his knees. "I would prefer to be master, with you as slave."

"And what would you order me to do?"

He was circling her as he spoke. She felt the slow, quiet, pantherlike prowl, the rake of his eyes on every inch of her form, and knew the hungry way he was eyeing her. She could literally feel the heavy longing in his gaze, every bit as exciting as the longing in his touch.

Her skin prickled with wanting. She felt the tingle as fine hairs stood up, and tiny beads of dampness danced to her skin's surface in unexpected places—the backs of her knees, the valley of her breasts, the top curve of her buttocks.

She caught her breath and licked her lips in anticipation. "What would I order you to do? Hmmmmm . . ."

Once more, she outlined her lips with the tip of her tongue. "First I would order you to disrobe. After that, I would have you brush my hair."

"Brush your hair?"

"It's a very pleasant sensation to have one's hair brushed. The roots are exceptionally sensitive. I love the way the scalp tingles."

Abruptly he placed his large, warm palm squarely on her mound. She felt the heat of him penetrate the thin silk, and shifted against him most wantonly to keep him off-balance. Let him think she would respond thus to any male who came within striking distance.

"Like this?" He spread his fingers wide, as if to encompass all of her feminine secrets. The heel of his hand pressed suggestively against her, enflaming her already overstimulated nubbin. She felt pinpricks of awareness up and down the insides of her legs.

"Not exactly the hair I was referring to, but resulting in a most a pleasant tingle nonetheless."

"Perhaps you should disrobe for me."

"I could. Should you choose to untie me," Aurora said.

"Ah, but whether you'd comply or not is another matter entirely. I have yet to see evidence to convince me you'll do my bidding."

"What evidence do you require?"

"No mind. I'm quite adept at taking matters into my own hands."

She felt the scrape of cold steel across her shoulders an instant before the knife blade severed the gown's straps and the transparent garment slithered from her body. As she felt it pool at her feet like a puddle of spilled cream, Aurora's excitement soared.

"I said I'd order *you* disrobed, not me."

"Role reversal," he said pleasantly. "What would you have your loyal slave do next?"

Aurora thought for a moment. "I would order you to make

love to me with your mouth. To kiss and lick and taste every scrap of my skin, beginning with my feet."

"Those are pretty big liberties for a stranger, don't you agree?"

"It's about my pleasure," Aurora said.

"So I am to bring you to ecstasy without taking my own ease, is that it?"

"Exactly," Aurora said.

"Role reversal," Grayson said, "means I fire you to a fever pitch, yet grant you no release."

"I doubt you have the skills," Aurora said, feigning bored tones. "Most men are intent only in serving their own needs, with scant regard for the woman."

"Says who?" he asked, clearly outraged by her statement.

"Women talk among themselves. The Rose and Thorn lot tend to be the most selfish of lovers. Or they drink too much till the alcohol impedes their performance, then lay blame on the woman for their inadequacies."

"You'll find there to be no inadequacies in this room."

"Really?" Aurora threw down her challenge like an invisible gauntlet. "So prove it."

"All in good time. Did we not agree the anticipation is part of the pleasure?"

"I didn't agree to a thing."

"Yet you stood on the auction floor among the other women, did you not? Took your chances on whom you would end up with for the night."

Aurora swallowed her smile of satisfaction hearing the ring of frustration in his voice. He was feeling unsure of her. "Life is a series of chances," she said gamely. "Lovers are pretty much interchangeable."

"We'll see about that. Are you ticklish?"

"Why do you want to know?"

She felt the soft brush of a feathery tip across the planes of her shoulders. It teased the underside of her arms, edged close to her breast, then slipped away. She felt the slow languorous journey of the feather caressing her spine, moving lower as it dipped into the crease of her behind. From there it slipped between her legs, floated effortlessly down the inside of one thigh, then up the other.

Aurora quivered from the teasing sensation, unwilling to reveal just how much she was enjoying their little game.

"What sort of lover requires props to please a woman?"

"The best sort. An imaginative lover."

"So you claim."

She heard his sharply indrawn breath and knew she was baiting him, pushing him. Knew he longed to kiss her, if only to silence her, quite certain he wondered if she had guessed his identity.

She let out a squeal of surprise as he cupped the cheeks of her derriere and squeezed. She felt his chest against her naked back as he molded his length to hers. His breath was hot in her ear as he spoke, his words so low, she had to strain her hearing to make them out.

"Such beautiful, unmarked white skin." He squeezed harder, rasped his fingernails across her buttocks. "I'm quite certain you've never tasted the lash of a whip."

He wouldn't dare!

Aurora turned her head toward him. His chin grazed her cheek. "It's only the weakest of men who resort to violent tactics in the bedroom."

"You have little idea of me or my tastes."

She gave his chin a playful nip with her teeth, then licked her teeth as if to savor his flavor. "You taste good to me."

He moved away abruptly. "You are naked and bound. Why are you not humble?"

"Perhaps because I am your equal, and we both know it."

"Perhaps because in reality I am your slave, and we both know that."

He moved in close again, fastened his lips to the back of her neck. She shuddered. Loosed a breathy sigh. Pulled at her bonds.

"Let me loose. Allow me to touch you as I long to."

"I like you at my mercy." He continued to attend her back, licking, tonguing, sucking, inflaming her with his hot, wet, deep kisses.

She moved against him, with him, craving more.

"Widen your stance."

She did as she was told. He reached the base of her spine and started on her buttocks, laving their rounded shape, outlining the dividing crease. Tracing the line, he probed and licked before he spread her cheeks and exposed the tiny mouth of her anus. Daintily, he dipped his tongue inside.

Aurora gasped. Her clit pulsed with an ache that only he could satisfy. She tried to press her legs tightly together for relief, but he pushed her legs farther apart.

"Stay like that," he ordered.

"And if I refuse?" She loved to taunt him. It heightened the fun of their game.

"I have ways to make you atone your disobedience."

He was back in a trice, and Aurora scarce dared to breathe, wondering what he was up to next.

She didn't have long to wait. She felt his fingers gliding between her rear cheeks again, getting her wetter still, then opening her, gently inserting something . . . Not his tongue, not his finger. Soft and wispy, yet solid, it filled her in a totally new way. Her excitement grew as she tried to imagine what he was about.

"I don't wish to hurt you. Tell me if that feels uncomfortable."

"It feels strange. An unusual fullness. I don't think I care for the sensation."

"Patience." He kissed her buttocks then, nibbled and licked and grazed like a hungry man. Her clit throbbed and pulsed, needing relief, stimulated by the unaccustomed full feeling and his risqué actions.

"Take it out," she said.

"Are you sure?"

"Yes. I told you I don't care for it."

"You don't know what it is."

"I'm not sure I want to know."

He slid around till his clever tongue began teasing her clit. She moaned aloud and quivered. So close, so ready, so ripe. As he licked, he made sharp tugging gestures behind, licking and tugging, front and back, in perfect harmony. The stimulation, so new and uncomfortable yet thrilling, built her desire to new heights.

Her orgasm, when it came, was more intense than any that had come before, and she stood shaking in the aftermath. Her legs were jelly. It was some time before she could speak.

"What was that device?"

"A knotted silk scarf—a most useful enhancement. Now what do you say about the selfishness of certain lovers?"

"I would have to exclude you from that lot. But I do not wish the other actresses to know, for they will all want their turn."

"If I were your slave, would you share me with the others?"

"Never," Aurora breathed. "I would insist on keeping you all to myself."

"Excellent. Now, here is the rest of your reward."

He reached around to the front of her and spread her open. She had never felt so helpless, so exposed, so vulnerable. The chilly air of the room against her overheated flesh fanned the flames of her desire and pushed her to new, uncharted heights.

Teasingly he stroked the crease at the top of her thighs, deliberately avoiding the spot where she needed his touch most.

Aurora gritted her teeth. She would not beg.

He continued to kiss and stroke and nibble and tease. She felt as if every inch of her was quivering. He ran his hands up and down her legs in a slow, insinuating fashion.

"Say you want me."

"You know I want you. My body burns for yours."

"I and I alone am the one who can satisfy you."

"Only you," Aurora said.

"You are my slave."

"You enslave me with more than these bonds or this mask."

"Would you like me to fuck you?"

"I would very much like you to make love to me."

"There is no difference."

"I beg to differ."

"Nonsense. 'Tis merely called lovemaking by the fairer sex to make the act of fornication more seemly."

"I disagree. The physical act involves only the body parts. The art of making love involves the mind as well as the body and lifts the couple to new heights of passion."

"And have you experienced such a thing? These new heights of passion to which you refer?"

"I have."

"How nice for you. But I only wish to fuck."

"It's impossible."

"I'll show you impossible!"

In a whirlwind of motion, he cut her loose and flung her on her back onto the bed. There was no gentleness in the way he roughly mounted her, then thrust himself inside of her in one swift motion. Yet her body knew his, welcomed his penetration, and she all but sobbed with relief that the torturous teasing neared its end.

Bucking and thrashing, she met his every frantic thrust with her own. If he thought to tame or subdue her with the force of his passion, he'd soon discover he'd once more met his match. Fast and frantic was their coupling, a tangle of arms and legs and sweat-sheened torsos.

"Kiss me," Aurora said.

"No kissing. We're fucking."

Every particle of her body sang with the rightness of his possession. If he expected her to try to soften the force of his ardor, he was sorely mistaken, for she loved the frantic energy of the ride, the way her body absorbed the impact of his thrusts, the full force of his possession in a way she'd never experienced before.

Grayson could think all he wanted that they were only rutting; her body knew the difference. And whether he admitted it or not, so did his.

She abruptly rolled and repositioned herself so she sat astride, leaned forward, and brushed his face with her breasts. "Suck my breasts," she ordered.

He stuck out his tongue and lashed them in unison. "I thought you were my slave."

"I tire of that role. Now you shall pleasure me—every way I say."

She rode him shallowly as he suckled her breasts, allowing his cock only an inch or so entrance at a time. She used him selfishly, rubbing herself with his velvet tip, inside and out, feeling her clit harden and pulse against him.

Then she moved forward, positioned herself directly over his face. "What else can you do with that tongue?" she purred, lowering her heat and brushing her female petals across his hot, hungry lips.

He moaned against her and buried his face in her softness.

His tongue and lips worked wicked pleasure and friction on her sensitive inner lips. He grasped her legs and spread them farther apart to allow himself greater access, as his tongue darted in and out of her like a miniature penis.

As she rode him, Aurora cupped her breasts in her hands, loving the way they responded to her touch, nipples budding and enhancing the pleasure of Grayson's many talents. She felt herself quicken, grasped the top of the headboard for support, and arched her back as wave after wave of orgasmic pleasure crashed through her. Finally spent, she collapsed weakly onto Grayson's chest.

"My turn." He grasped her hips and settled her upon his straining cock. She moaned deeply and caught his fire as he once more joined with her, rendering them one.

Their minds and bodies meshed as they moved together, loved together; both striving to reach, yet somehow delay, the inevitable culmination of their passion. Just as Aurora felt the beginning of her next orgasm meet the beginning of his, Grayson ripped off her mask and captured her lips with his.

And their hungry kiss melded them, pushing each other over the top into new echelons of carnal bliss.

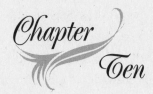

Chapter Ten

"*Aurora.*" She felt Grayson shake her bare shoulder and nudge her slowly awake.

"What is it?"

"Nearly dawn. Your special time."

"Mmmmmmm." She rolled over and tried to bury her head in the pillow, but he persevered, continuing to shake her till she roused.

"Come. I have a surprise. It's something you won't want to miss."

He was already dressed to ride, she saw, as she struggled to swing still-liquid limbs over the edge of the bed. The room was bathed in early-morning gray; dawn had not yet sprinkled her magic half-light. Aurora rubbed her eyes. A woman's riding suit had been laid out across a nearby chair.

"The room is like ice," she said as she pushed back the covers and rose with one last longing glance at the warm bed.

"We won't be here long enough to necessitate lighting the fire."

As she quickly dressed in the clothes, he faced away from her, rummaging through a bureau drawer.

She knew the second something was amiss. His movements froze. He appeared to hold his breath as he stiffly turned to face her.

"What? What's the matter?" Aurora raced to his side.

Both hands were clenched into tight fists. "What makes you think something is the matter?"

"Oh, for pity's sake, Grayson. Do you really believe for an instant that I'm not privy to your moods and reactions? I know something is wrong the same way I knew from the outset it was you who claimed me last night."

"Yet you never let on."

"What? And ruin your little game?"

He eyed her coolly. "You enjoy believing you hold the upper hand, don't you?"

Men! Aurora resisted the urge to roll her eyes. "When it comes to us, neither holds one hand over the other. The cards seem equally dealt." She reached for him, tugged on his arm. "Show me what has you so perturbed."

Slowly he unclenched a fist to reveal a silver ring nested against his palm. She recognized it instantly.

"Your Rose and Thorn ring."

"Not mine. Someone else's."

Her eyes widened as she noted the place where the rose petals had broken off the face of the ring.

"What does it mean?"

He tucked the ring in his pocket.

"It means whoever killed my father is more cunning than I suspected."

A thoughtful silence stretched between them as she quickly finished dressing, pondering this new development, then followed him through the sleeping house to the stables.

" 'Tis still dark." She spoke breathlessly, at a half run to keep abreast of Grayson's long-legged stride.

"See how the dawn has just barely started to lighten the horizon, heralding a new day."

"The last day," Aurora said, in a subdued tone. *Our* last day.

"One you won't want to miss a moment of."

A sleepy-looking groom held the reins of two horses, saddled and ready. Grayson helped her onto a dappled gray before he mounted his own black stallion. Only then did he turn, and ask, "I trust you can ride?"

Typical Grayson, Aurora thought. Do first, ask about it second. "I confess it's been some time." She attempted to get a comfortable grip on her reins while the groom adjusted her stirrups.

Grayson lowered his voice so that none could hear, save her. "I trust you're not too sore to ride?"

Aurora laughed. Should she be touched by his thoughtfulness or scandalized at the implication? "Certainly not!" Even should she be too tender to sit a saddle, she'd die rather than admit it.

As they started from the barn, Aurora slowly rediscovered her pleasure in riding. Her skills might be rusty but weren't lost. Her mount was a delight. As if having sensed Aurora's hesitancy at first, the gray responded accordingly, giving Aurora time to find the familiar rhythm of a saddle beneath her.

Grayson glanced over his shoulder toward her. "All right?"

"More than all right." She drew a deep, appreciative breath. The sunrise cast its brilliance upon the land, and the energy that accompanied the start of a new day was positively invigorating. Her mount followed the stallion as if she had no other purpose and total trust in the bigger horse's lead. Matched by Aurora's equal trust in the rider, although it had taken her a while to acknowledge it. She smiled at her thoughts. Perhaps animals really did know best.

Gray turned at that exact moment and caught his breath at the radiance of her expression—as if Aurora herself represented the dawnlight that illuminated his life.

He frowned. Admittedly she was refreshing and intriguing, as well as inspiring. She was also a distraction. In her presence, the drive to find his father's killer, while in no way diminished, did seem to lessen in importance.

"What are you planning to do next?"

He cast her an exasperated look. On the surface, it was a general-enough question. In actual fact, it was as if she had reached into his brain and plucked out his thoughts, making them also her own.

"There are other clues besides the ring," he said brusquely.

"Such as?" She cantered the short distance to reach his side. He liked her being next to him. A little too much.

"Aurora, do you never cease to chatter? As well as to blunder in on those things that are none of your concern," he said in a steely tone.

Aurora sat up straighter, thrust her chest out, and tilted her head at a belligerent angle. "There was a time not too long past when you commended me for my lack of chatter. This morn, those things which concern you are my concern, as well."

"This has naught to do with you. I'm sorry I ever confided in you."

"But you didn't—I guessed, didn't I? I knew something was on your mind, and I ferreted it out. If I'd waited on your confidence, I'd be waiting still."

He pulled up short. She did likewise.

"You are impossible!"

She dimpled, seeming quite pleased with his show of temper. "Thank you. I consider that very much a compliment. Who in their right mind would want to be labeled 'possible'?"

"I don't know if I want to shake you or to kiss you," Gray admitted.

She leaned toward him. "You've tried both. The kissing is infinitely more fun."

He accepted her challenge. Leaning forward, he brushed her lips with his own. "Good morning."

"Good morning, yourself," she said, her breath a sweet warm caress across his face.

"I apologize for my temper. You do have a way of getting under my skin."

"I'll choose to take that as a compliment, as well. Thank you for arranging this sunrise ride. It's something I'll always remember."

"Come this way," he said, preparing to move forward. "I have one more thing for the memory store."

Her hand on his arm stopped him. "I fear my senses are already overloaded. Look at that!"

Her sweeping gaze included the full spectrum of their surroundings. The way a stream lazily wended its way through grassy fields bordered by a copse of trees, intersected by the occasional fence or hedgerow, as a sweeping palette of colors slashed across the royal blue morning sky. Tangerine and persimmon shades were undertoned by scarlet and gold.

"Can we stay still for a moment? I don't want to blink, in case I miss something more wonderful than what just passed."

As always, her enthusiasm was contagious. Before he met Aurora, when had he ever slowed down enough to enjoy, to savor, to drink in the many splendors afforded by nature?

"Of course we can. My surprise isn't going anywhere." Gray could hardly credit the sound of his own voice—soft, patient, amused. Aurora had introduced not just a way of viewing life differently, but a means to experience it differently. As if he'd viewed his surroundings in shades of black or white before, and now she had introduced him to color, exposed him to flavors and textures hitherto unrecognized. As a general rule he was focused, firmly intent on the destination rather than the journey. Today he was full-on enveloped by the journey.

He swung out of the saddle and reached her side before she even noticed, then claimed her reins and held out his arms for her to dismount.

She gave him a far-too-all-seeing look as she slid from her saddle into his waiting arms. "I thought you were hell-bent on getting somewhere specific."

"A change of mind is not a privilege reserved solely for women, you know."

What of a change of heart? She cocked her head to one side and studied him with an intensity he found unnerving. "I would have guessed that once your mind is set a certain way, nothing causes it to change. Which makes your name delightfully ironic."

He cleared his throat. "Why would you say that?"

She laughed, a melodious sound that the breeze tossed about in gay abandon. "People who know you well call you Gray, but there is nothing gray in your view. Things are either black or they're white. So a man named Gray who doesn't see anything as gray . . ."

"Life is simpler in black and white," he said gruffly.

"Who concluded life was ever simple?" she asked scoffingly. "Myself, I've found it to be damnably complex."

"Ladies ought not to swear."

She dropped a mocking curtsy, hands folded as in prayer before her. "Am I allowed to sit, oh great and powerful master?"

"You enjoy teasing me, don't you?"

"Grayson, I enjoy you as you enjoy me. Whether it be teasing or seducing, or . . ." Impishly she plucked a stem of wild grass and tickled his ear with its plumelike tip. In spite of himself, he shied away.

Her grin widened. "Don't tell me you're ticklish? How have I not discovered that before now?"

"Only sometimes," Gray said.

"Really? Exactly where and when, I wonder? After we make love, when your skin is all tingly and every part of you is oversensitized?"

He pulled the grass from her grasp and tossed it over his shoulder. "You are a most difficult woman." Then he pulled her to him and kissed her, well aware he'd not want her any other way. He felt the sun on his head, smelled the sunshine and sweet wild grass, heard the faint gurgle of water in the distance. In the sheltering circle of his arms Aurora quivered, sighed, and shifted closer, fitting herself to him. He gathered her nearer still.

When had a woman ever managed to get this close? Not merely in the physical sense, but on a mental level, as well. The knowledge that someone knew him so intimately inside as well as out . . . It was intoxicating, yet at the same time it triggered a myriad of internal warning bells.

Aurora was one hell of an actress. Perhaps he was simply part of the performance. A walk-on.

He didn't want to believe that. As he tumbled her hair loose and drank the sweetness she offered, he realized how bereft his life had been before her arrival. Even now, the memory of her hopping out of that balloon, champagne glass in hand, had the power to make him smile.

She drew back slightly. "What's so funny?"

"How did you know I was smiling? I thought you were swooning from my kiss."

"I don't swoon," she said forcefully. "And I know you."

"Damned if you don't," he said ruefully. "So tell me, what was I thinking about just now that made me smile?"

"I expect you were thinking about me. I do believe I make you smile like no one else ever has."

He nuzzled her forehead. "That makes us even. For I do believe I've made you come like no one else ever has."

"You've shown me passion in all its many guises, masked and unmasked," she replied.

"And if I profess to be not yet quite finished in that regard?"

"Please, sir, take pity on the maid starved for your touch."

She spoke of starvation, Gray thought as he stripped off his jacket and spread it on the grass near his feet, yet he was the one who'd been half-starved. Living a life that only pretended to be full and richly satisfying.

"Do you wish to sit, madam?" He indicated his waiting jacket with a flourish. She doffed her own jacket and spread it next to his. "I'm thinking we might need a little more room."

"What did you have in mind?"

"I'm quite certain our minds are traveling in the same direction," she said. Settling herself, she lost no time in removing her boots and stockings, wiggling her bare toes in happy abandon in the sunshine. "That feels infinitely better."

She stretched back, arms behind her, and raised her face to the sun.

Gray knelt alongside her. "Do that again."

"What? This?" She wiggled her bare toes. "Or this?" She arched her back, thrusting her breasts upward.

"All of it," Gray said as he pounced upon her, his body stretched atop hers.

She linked her hands behind his head and brought his mouth within kissing distance. "This has truly been an adventure of the finest order."

He eluded her kiss. "Is that what I am to you? Just one in a series of grand adventures? Any day now, will you balloon off into some new adventure?"

"We could have an adventure together," she said. "Rebuild the Gaslight Theater to her former splendor."

"I intend to tear it down."

"Grayson." She slid one hand down the length of his spine, and he could feel the sear of her touch through his shirt. "Give the theater a chance."

He heard everything she wasn't saying. *Give us a chance.*

The words hung between them with the fragility of a spider's web. One wrong move from either, and they would be swept from existence forever.

Had he ever been so torn? On the one hand, he longed to see her face alight with animation, to watch her scheme and plan with keen enthusiasm, joining in where needed. But that theater had destroyed everything he'd ever held near and dear. He would not allow it to destroy Aurora.

"It's impossible," he said.

"Grayson, nothing is impossible."

Damn her, she made it sound so easy.

"I've seen too much to believe in the truth of that."

Her hand slipped from his back to his arm, her touch the lightest, most soothing of caresses. As if she knew, without words, the conflict roiling through him. The responsibilities he had yet to see to. The answers he required.

"You've had your answer," he said harshly. "I've said no to the theater."

"In that case, I wager there's a good chance you'll say yes to me." Her turn to pounce this time, to straddle him, one bent leg on either side of his hips. Her breasts strained against the confines of her blouse, begging for his attention. He could feel the womanly juncture of her legs and knew he could lose himself in her. With her.

He wouldn't be the weak man his father had been and lose himself with a woman. Had he perhaps spoken aloud? For she touched his lips with the tip of her finger. When she spoke, her words were so soft he had to strain to catch them. He wondered if perhaps he imagined the entire situation. Or if perhaps they spoke with no words. Spoke what was in their hearts.

"You won't lose yourself with me, Grayson. 'Tis the way you'll find yourself again."

He wanted to believe her. Oh, how he wanted to believe the truth in her words.

He reached up and unbuttoned her blouse with reverent slowness. So slowly that she pushed his hands out of the way and took over the task. He enjoyed the sight of her, fingers trembling with impatience as she bared the feasts of nature's bounty. Creamy shoulders. Plunging décolletage.

"May I?" He plucked at the lacing on the front of her deliciously feminine lace-edged camisole.

"Of course."

"My pleasure."

"And mine," she said, her voice a throaty purr.

Before he put pressure on the lacing, he leaned forward and kissed her on the sensitive, curving spot where shoulder meets neck—one of his favorite places of the female anatomy, because it was so surprising, so incredibly responsive. He touched it lightly with the tip of his tongue and felt her pulse leap in response. He circled his tongue in ever-widening sweeps before he branded her skin with his lips and drank deeply her sweet essence.

She moaned and melted against him.

He attacked the laces then, freed her breasts and availed himself of the pleasure of just touching her and absorbing her rapture, her instant response like fire in his blood.

She moved against him. "That makes me so wet."

"I know," he said. "I can feel it."

"I want you."

"And so you shall have me. All in good time."

Unexpectedly she pushed him backward, and he lost his balance. Beneath her he lay while she rubbed her heated mound back and forth on the ridge of his erect penis. The layers of clothing between them acted more as enticement than deterrent. He felt her heat, her wanting, and the knowledge stirred him to greater excitement.

She moved over him, dragging her unbound breasts across his chin and cheeks, just slightly out of reach of his greedy mouth and tongue. At the same time her hot mound pivoted against his hips, seeking and finding his hardened length.

One pass of her breasts swept near enough that he could close his mouth around a turgid nipple and suck gently, deeply. He felt a fresh outpouring of heat from her and nearly lost it in a way he hadn't since he was in short pants.

"Enough!" He reached up, grasped her bare shoulders, and physically inserted distance between them.

"Enough?" she echoed, clearly disappointed. "We've only just begun."

"*You* may have only just begun. It was nearly all over for me, and that is not a boyhood memory I care to revisit."

"What, making a mess in your clothing?" she asked with mock innocence.

"It would be difficult to explain to Hudson," Gray said.

"We can't be upsetting Hudson, now can we? Best if you were to remove that pesky clothing."

"Your thoughts parallel mine exactly."

And when they were both unclothed and unfettered, smiled down upon by lady sun, they came together, their coupling no less intense for the rhythm of slow, sure strokes with which he filled her and she welcomed him.

He raised himself up onto his elbows so he could enjoy the sheer ecstasy crossing her face as her first orgasm hit. He pushed back her hair, tangling his hands in its rich fullness, loving the breathless, quivering noises she made while her body gloved his in liquid heat.

She arched her back so her breasts tickled his chest, and he couldn't resist darting down to tease—first one nipple, then the other, laving their responsive peaks, coaxing them to delightful marblelike hardness as he drew them deep inside his mouth.

She sighed at the sensation, and the sound ricocheted through him, spreading her pleasure in his actions. He embedded himself deep within and moved from side to side with ever-widening strokes. Strokes she met and matched with her own rhythm, designed to heighten her pleasure and his.

Perhaps it was the simple act of being outdoors in the daylight, or perhaps it was simply Aurora herself, and her unabashed pleasure derived from their joining. But as he felt her quicken and her muscles tighten around him, signaling the next round of her letting go, the next level of her journey up the heights to which he piloted her, he wondered. Their lovemaking seemed different. No less pleasurable in its intensity, but a slow burn, rather than a wildfire. The kind of flames on which one can build for a lifetime. It was a sobering thought.

Slowly and carefully he made love to her as if she were as precious, fragile, and fleeting as the dawn of her name. Come the morrow, she'd be naught but a memory. And his days could well sink into permanent darkness, denied her ready smile, quick wit, and sensual body.

She, too, seemed to sense a faint air of bitter sweetness in the coupling, for she slowed her movements to match his. Scaling the heights and reaching for new ones, she clung to him, a sudden fierceness in her grip, as if she would never willingly be the first to let go.

BY THE TIME THEY reached his surprise it wasn't much of a surprise, for the sound gave it away long before they were within sight of the waterfall.

"This is the source of the water that's diverted to the pond and fountains on the estate," Gray said.

Next to him, Aurora stared openmouthed in awe. And with her by his side he observed it as if for the first time. It was an impressive sight, the way water crashed over cliffs thirty feet high, pooled at the base, then marshaled its energy in a race to points west. The sun's rays sparked rainbows through the fine spray of mist on the edges of the falls.

"I've never seen a waterfall up close before," Aurora said in a hushed tone.

Gray dismounted and held a hand to help her down. "Shall we?"

She dismounted as well and leaned against him, making no move to step from the sheltering circle of his arms.

"It's truly amazing," Aurora breathed.

He bit back the instinct to make the same claim regarding her.

His mount chose that moment to sniff the air and let out a snort, Gray's cue to release Aurora and secure both their horses to a nearby tree.

Then he caught Aurora's hand in his. "We can walk up through this way and stand behind it, if you wish."

"Grayson, can we really?"

As always, Aurora's enthusiasm was infectious. Keeping a firm hold on her, he led the way to the hidden trail that wound up and around to the shallow cave in back of the waterfall.

Another woman might have been put off by the roughness of the climb or shied away from the dark, damp cavern and its slimy, moss-covered walls and the deafening noise from the falls.

Aurora reacted like a small child who had stumbled across St. Nicholas's workshop. Nothing would do but to explore every nook and cranny behind the falls. She even removed her riding gloves and stretched out her hands to capture the falls' moisture and splash it on her face.

"Don't go too close to the edge," he warned, raising his voice in order to be heard. "The rocks are slippery."

She nodded gravely and took a step back, closer to him. Her obedience gave him pause.

He'd already told her "no" on the theater. And he knew firsthand that she didn't take no for an answer—witness her tenacity to seek an audience with him. Was she planning similar tactics to make him change his mind? Was that the motivating factor behind her enthusiastic coupling? If Aurora thought to use her feminine charms to change his mind, she was due for a deep disappointment. He'd never succumb.

And more importantly, he had a killer to unmask.

"We should be getting back."

He didn't realize until he spoke just how closely she had been watching him. She'd been uncommonly quiet and her face wore a thoughtful expression, slightly troubled.

She placed a hand against his cheek in a soothing gesture. "You look far too serious. This is a party, after all."

"Yes," he said harshly. "And one of the guests is a killer."

"Do you fear for your own safety? And that of your guests?"

"I'm not sure of his or her motives. Or how they might react should someone suddenly get in their way."

Aurora nodded, her mood clearly as subdued as his. Yet, Aurora being Aurora, she didn't stay subdued for long. No sooner had they returned to where they'd left the horses, than she scampered off to the edge of the pool beneath the falls. He followed in time to see her ripping off her stockings and boots.

"The water's like ice," he said.

"I know. But it's so beautiful here. I shall simply pretend we're in a rain forest, surrounded by tropical birds and plants, and that the water is bubbling up from a nearby hot springs at bath temperature." In a trice she had abandoned her riding skirt and waded in up to her knees.

He wanted to be the one accompanying her to that rain forest—and all the other wonders of the world. "Bath temperature, is it?"

"Not quite," Aurora admitted. "Come try for yourself."

"I prefer to leave my trousers on, thank you."

"I've seen evidence otherwise." Her tone was as teasing as her expression, provocative and innocently seductive. His body responded in typical fashion. Had he ever known such a woman? She was an enticing mix of worldliness and naïveté. Seductress and inexperience. Perhaps, after all, not all women were cut from the same mold as Celeste.

She laughed at him, sent a splash his way, only to have it miss its mark by a wide margin. She laughed and tried again.

She looked like a comely water sprite cavorting in the forest pool. A ray of sunlight glanced off her hair and turned it to liquid golden fire, all but blinding in its brilliance.

As he was committing to memory the picture she presented, a gunshot abruptly punctured the silence.

Both horses reared up and whinnied in terror.

Gray splashed through the pool, scooped Aurora into his arms, and carried her to cover. He tossed her down behind a thicket and shielded her body with his own, cursing himself for putting her in harm's way.

He could taste her fear, hear the frantic beat of her heart beneath his own, even as she strove to keep her tone light.

"Do you think that was deliberate?"

Gray hoped she didn't detect the lie in his voice. "Most likely it was some careless hunter who realized his mistake and took off."

"Are the horses all right?"

"They're spooked."

Aurora forced a laugh. "Can't say I blame them for that."

Gray cast his eye across the landscape for signs of movement, but there were none. All was still. Birds chattered, the falls cascaded, the stream gurgled.

Too late, he recalled the way Diablo had shifted restlessly as he tied him up, had whinnied in slight uneasiness. Warning signs he ought to have recognized yet had ignored, distracted by Aurora. The woman was more than clouding his judgment. She was proving a liability in his life, all around.

Even now, stretched beneath him half-clothed, he could feel her heat, smell her distinctive fragrance. A smell that would haunt him forever. Along with his memories of her.

He spoke abruptly. “I’m sending you back to the city.”

Chapter Eleven

Grayson loomed above her, large and vital and fiercely protective, and her heart swelled with love and longing till she felt something inside might burst. She could barely breathe for the weight of the emotions inside her, let alone think.

She didn't hear him say he was sending her away. She heard her lover desperate to protect her, to keep her safe. And in that moment, she knew she loved Grayson more than she had ever dreamed it possible to love another.

Naturally she couldn't allow him to send her away. She'd stay for as long as it took and help in any way possible while Grayson unmasked his father's killer.

Knowing her father had taken his own life, it had been difficult holding her head up against the public censure. How awful for Grayson to suffer that same public judgment, knowing for a fact his father had not died by his own hand.

She felt Grayson shift till he was kneeling next to her. When he passed her a pistol, she blinked. Where had that come from?

"Take this. Sit tight. If anything moves out there, anything at all, shoot it."

"I want to go with you."

"Don't worry, I'll be back. I'm just taking a look around."

"But—"

"Aurora, for once would you at least pretend to follow instructions?"

She fell silent. Did Grayson really think her so uncooperative? He slipped silently through the underbrush, and she propped herself up on her elbows, eyes narrowed, as she kept a vigilant watch of her surroundings.

She glanced at the gun she held awkwardly in both her hands. There had seemed no point in telling Gray she'd never fired one before and most likely couldn't hit the broad side of a barn. She started, hearing an unfamiliar birdcall. Wasn't that sometimes the way robbers signaled each other when the coast was clear?

Silly. There were no robbers out here. Nothing to steal except the horses, which were well out of sight.

Everything sounded overly loud in the slowly waking morning countryside, and Aurora knew her imagination was working overtime. Surely that was just a twig snapping, not a stealthy footfall. She was just conjuring sounds up out of nothing. Still, she couldn't shake that eerie feeling of being watched. The feeling, which had been very real the other night at the mansion, was equally strong today.

Gray made a thorough examination of the surrounding countryside, where he found unmistakable signs that he and Aurora had been followed. Someone had been out here on horseback this morning besides them. He was angry with himself for not noticing. If he weren't so damn distracted by Aurora, he would have. Instead, he'd inadvertently put her in danger.

Finally convinced that whoever had followed them was no longer in the area, he returned to where he'd left the horses, untied them, and made his way back to Aurora.

It ought to be a relatively simple matter to find out who else had taken a horse from the stables this morning. But life was rarely as simple as it ought to be, which had him worried.

"Don't shoot, Aurora. It's just me."

He entered the hiding place only to find it empty.

"Up here," Aurora called.

He followed the direction of her voice. Branches moved, leaves rustled, and Aurora came into view. Crazy woman.

"What are you doing up there?"

"Keeping a lookout. I could swear I felt someone watching me. It was creepy."

"If anyone was out there," Gray kept his voice deliberately casual, "he or she has long gone."

He had to admit to enjoying the view as Aurora gracefully clambered down from her perch. She reached his side and pulled the pistol from the waistband of her knickers. "Is it safe for me to go fetch my skirt?"

"If you feel so inclined. I have to say, though, you look remarkably fetching in your unmentionables."

They reached the estate with no further incidents or encounters with stray bullets, yet she knew as soon as they entered the stables that something was wrong. No groom arrived to greet them and attend to their mounts.

Grayson helped her down.

"Go over to the house, Aurora. I'll get to the bottom of this."

"I'm tired of you constantly ordering me out of the way. I'm as much a part of this as you are."

"That's where you're mistaken. Now kindly heed my wishes. Eat a hearty breakfast and stay in your room until I fetch you."

Send her back to the city is what he meant.

That's when she heard the moan. Together they hurried to a nearby stall, where they found the groom rubbing his eyes and struggling to his feet.

"Tim, are you hurt? What happened?"

"I'm not sure, Mr. Grayson. After you two left, I had my porridge. I was starting to do my work when suddenly I felt powerfully sleepy. I don't recall another thing till just now."

Clearly the man had been drugged. Aurora opened her mouth to say as much, but was stopped by a single look from Grayson.

"Not to worry," Grayson said, making light of the incident. "Could you see to our horses, please?"

"Certainly, Mr. Grayson."

"Why didn't you say something?" Aurora asked, once they were out of earshot. "He deserves to know what happened."

"We don't know what happened; we're only guessing. The less said about any of this, the better. I'll see you at the house in short order."

Aurora was far from happy at being dismissed again, like so much window dressing. Didn't Grayson realize that she had a brain in her head? That together, two heads were far better than one?

Aurora found she had very little appetite for Mrs. Blossom's delicious breakfast offerings. She sipped at her tea and picked at her scone, leaving much more on her plate than she managed to force down her throat.

She was totally consumed with devising a plan to stay, despite Grayson's insistence she leave within the hour. No doubt he intended to bundle her into the carriage himself, and she had naught of any value with which to bribe the driver, even if she could convince him to let her off a short distance from the estate.

"Why so deep in thought, she of the fiery hair and matching temper?"

She glanced up to see Grayson's brother, Beau.

"Not all women have fluff for brains," she muttered darkly.

"You mean some women are capable of thoughts deeper than the latest fashion or the weather?"

"Indeed. You're up early."

"I believe the early bird catches the worm, is the expression? Not that I was out for worms this morning."

Upon closer look, Aurora saw he had several fresh-looking scratches along one cheek. "Were you out riding?" she asked casually. "Beautiful morning for it."

"Afraid not. That would require considerable more energy than I'm willing to expend."

"What do you do with your time here in the country?" Aurora asked.

"Very little, I'm happy to report." Beau reached past her for the marmalade and butter.

"Don't you find the time hangs heavily on your hands? Does Grayson give you things to see to on the estate?"

"My esteemed big brother? Heavens, no. He's only happy when he has all of the control."

"Surely you would prefer to earn your own keep."

Beau laughed. "Why? As Celeste's son, I'm a Grayson also. Graysons need do nothing other than play if they so choose."

"Your mother still acts onstage."

"That's her version of play. Just as acting the lord of the manor is Grayson's favorite pastime."

Aurora took a sip of her tea, wondering if Beau had the inner workings to be a killer. Perhaps with Grayson's father out of the picture, he'd get more attention.

"I have means," Aurora said. "Money left me by my late husband. Do you have means, or are you dependent upon Grayson?"

"Mother makes certain I feel independent of my brother."

Not much motive there for murder, Aurora thought. "Don't you feel the urge to accomplish something with your life?"

"Good Lord. Whatever for? I quite embrace being a ne'er-do-well younger brother and an embarrassment to Gray."

"I wouldn't think your brother would embarrass any too easily."

"Well, that's true enough. He considers himself well above the rest of us."

Watching Beau take his leave, Aurora saw a sad and lonely young man desperate for attention from an absentee mother and a disinterested older brother. How far might he go to gain attention?

Reluctantly she rose from the table. Grayson would expect to find her in her room, meekly waiting, and she knew he'd not take kindly to any effort to defy him.

She could always attempt to disappear someplace on the estate, but knew he'd turn over every stick and stone on the place till he found her, a distraction he didn't need. He needed to be ferreting out the identity of his father's killer, not looking for her.

But how could she leave, when she so wanted to help him? Her heart was as heavy as her tread as she made her way up the stairs and down the hall to Celeste's room.

"Psstt!"

Aurora stopped and glanced around, hearing the whispered summons from a shadowy doorway.

"Who is it?" she whispered back. "Who's there?"

A cloaked and hooded figure stepped from the shadows and approached Aurora furtively, glancing over her shoulder as if fearing to be set upon at any second.

"Misty?"

"Aurora, I need your help." The other woman's voice quavered with uncertainty, her words barely audible.

Aurora gave a quick glance in both directions. "In here." She whisked her friend into her room and locked the door behind them.

Once they were safely inside, Misty let the hood of her cloak slide from her head and slowly turned to face her. Aurora gasped. One eye was black-and-blue and swollen half-shut. Misty's lower lip was puffed to twice its normal size, marred by traces of dried blood.

Misty met her horrified gaze. "You're not seeing the worst of it, believe me."

"Who did this?"

"Whoever bought me from the auction last night. I don't know who he was; he made a point not to reveal his identity. But I can't possibly stay here any longer."

"I'll help you get away," Aurora said. "If I can't figure something out, Grayson will. He'd never sanction this type of behavior."

"Don't be too sure," Misty said darkly. "Lots of these gents have a dark side. 'Tis part of the attraction of the Rose and Thorn—the anonymity."

"Speaking of anonymity, the members are all supposed to wear their rings. Ever notice anyone wearing a ring with part of the rose missing?"

Misty's gaze grew guarded. "Maybe. Why?"

"Misty, it's important. Do you know who?"

"I don't want to get anyone in trouble."

"Why would you get him into trouble?"

"He's not really a member, but sometimes he shows up wearing a ring."

"Who? Who's not a member?"

Misty gave a deep sigh. "It's Grayson's half brother. Beauregard."

"Beau? You're sure?"

"Aurora, don't say anything unless you need to, please? I feel sorry for the bloke. He wants so bad to fit in, to belong someplace."

"Do you know whose ring he borrows?"

Misty shook her head slowly as if it hurt to do so. "I never asked him, never let on I knew who he was. Or that he wasn't one of the club."

"Do you think maybe it was he who beat you up?" Aurora asked. Beau had been sporting those fresh scratches; they could have been from a woman's fingernails.

"I honestly can't say one way or another."

"What happens tonight?" Aurora asked. "The last night."

"We actresses have been rehearsing a stage play to get the gents fired up. But I can't go on like this, even if I wanted to. I'm too marked up."

And too afraid, Aurora knew.

"Don't worry about the play. Right now, we need to get you away from here—and I believe I have the answer."

Aurora was encased in Misty's travel cloak when Grayson

arrived at her door and escorted her outside to where a carriage and driver stood waiting. She flung herself into his arms, hoping she wasn't overacting the part of a woman who might never see her lover again.

For his part, Grayson barely acknowledged her presence or her performance. He looked grim, giving her cause to wonder what he had unearthed. Whatever his discovery, it was quite clearly nothing he was willing to share.

"I'll be in touch." He handed her into the carriage hastily, as if he couldn't wait to see the end of her, and stood in the drive observing her retreat. The moment they rounded a bend and were out of sight, Aurora stuck her head out the window and got the driver's attention.

"I'm so terribly sorry. I seem to have forgotten my jewelry box. Could we possible nip back so I can get it?"

The driver was no doubt used to flighty female guests on the estate, for he appeared resigned as he drew the horses to a stop.

"Don't bother to turn the carriage around. I'll just hasten back on foot and return before you even notice."

"Very good, Miss. I'll wait right here."

At their prearranged meeting place, halfway down the drive, she met Misty, and they exchanged cloaks. Misty carried a small traveling bag in one hand. As she pulled the hood up over her head, she gave Aurora a quick hug.

"I'll not forget this."

"Everything will work out just fine, you'll see," Aurora said, wishing that she actually believed her own words.

Hugging the shadows, she returned to the mansion.

Stealthily she slipped into the kitchen and up the back staircase to her room, where she set about learning her role for the evening's play. 'Twas like no play she had ever been in before. There were no lines to learn, only marks to hit. She just hoped she was a good enough actress to mount a credible performance.

RANDALL STROLLED INTO Gray's study. "The man is here to set the fireworks for tonight, Gray. Where do you want him?"

"Bloody hell," Gray said. "Is it too late to consign the entire crew to some other poor sod's estate?"

"They'll be on their way tomorrow."

"Can't happen soon enough for me."

"What of the widow Tremblay?"

"Safely on her way back to San Francisco some hours ago."

"I saw your dispatch ride in. Did you receive the word you'd been waiting for?"

"Finally," Gray said. "Details from the mortgagor of the theater. The fellow picked a damned inopportune time to travel extensively abroad."

"I take it you have your next move plotted?"

"As always, timing is of the essence," Gray said. "I just have to get through this wretched performance tonight, then all will be resolved."

"I'll help our man get things set up," Randall said with a cheeriness Gray could only envy. "Onward, upward, and all that."

"Be careful of those explosives," Gray said. "I'd appreciate you staying all in one piece."

"Why, Grayson," Randall mocked, "a bloke might think you've gotten soft in your old age."

Gray snorted at Randall's retreating back, but his friend's words gave him pause. Had Aurora had a softening influence? Thank goodness she was safely away before the evening's grand finale, one less thing for him to worry about. Once this Rose and Thorn debacle was a thing of the past and the cloud over his father's death satisfied . . .

He caught his thoughts midstream. By then, Aurora would be off chasing some new adventure. She'd have forgotten all about her fleeting visit to the Grayson Estate.

AURORA FOLLOWED MISTY'S detailed instructions as she donned her costume and prepared to step further back into the world of make-believe. The entire time at Grayson Estate had been more a dream than reality. So much had happened in so short a time, she could scarcely believe she was the same person who had so boldly dropped into Grayson's life three days earlier.

Studying her reflection in the looking glass only accentuated how much had changed, including Aurora herself. For she'd fallen hopelessly in love with a man who, right now, seemed as distant and unattainable as the moon. Thank goodness there was no chance of his recognizing her onstage tonight.

The costume wasn't much of a costume at all, for its sole purpose was to have it appear as if the wearer was naked. Misty had assured her all the girls would be dressed identically. Aurora sighed as she wrestled her uncooperative hair up under the dark wig and donned the brightly jeweled mask. She felt like a different person, and it was no longer a comfortable feeling. She liked being Aurora Tremblay. And she particularly enjoyed the feeling of being in love.

She glanced out the window to the courtyard, where a makeshift stage had been erected, and wished with all her heart she didn't have to be part of the performance. She was tired of pretending to be someone she wasn't.

With Grayson she'd learned to be totally herself, and it was a feeling she longed to embrace forever. He accepted her completely, didn't expect her to change or act a certain way to suit his needs. It was so freeing. Love, which she'd always thought to be utterly confining, had turned out the exact opposite.

As Aurora prepared to go downstairs, she heard a loud crack like a gunshot. Surely not again?

Her sole thought was Grayson's safety as she raced outside to where the night air rang with what sounded like an entire volley of gunshots. She burst into the courtyard and froze, for the sky was ablaze with showers of light and color. Glittering rainbows fell through the night air and illuminated the courtyard like magic.

Fireworks! What else had Misty neglected to mention about the evening ahead?

As she stood staring up in wonder of the display, she found herself once more subject to that uncomfortable feeling of being observed. As the fireworks died off, smoke lingered heavily in the air, over which Aurora swore she could smell the pungent scent of a cigar. She had to get away.

Inside the ballroom, Aurora found herself immediately

drawn into the backstage hubbub she recalled so well. Girls flitted to and fro in a precurtain frenzy. As she looked around, she saw one other detail Misty had neglected to mention. The other costumes were in color. Hers was the only one fashioned to resemble bare skin.

"Come over here, Misty. Let me finish off your costume."

One of the girls grabbed a stick of black greasepaint and drew a crude thatch at the juncture of Aurora's thighs. Red greasepaint was used to outline the orbs of her nipples, and before she could voice a protest, she heard the band strike up.

"There's our cue. Ready?"

"Almost." Aurora grabbed a nearby glass of champagne and downed it in a swallow before she turned to take her place in the line.

The band belted out "Street of Cairo," a bump and grind number, as the girls made their way up the steps and hootchy-kootchied across the stage. Several servants were lighting torches across the front of the stage for illumination. Aurora was on last. She took a breath and bravely stepped forward toward the one and only prop, a long dining table draped in a sheet.

GRAY STOOD TO ONE SIDE of the stage, rather than surging forward to ogle with the rest of the men. As the actresses appeared one by one in their skimpy and suggestive costumes, he'd expected to feel disgust.

Disgust for the men who encouraged and enjoyed this type of performance, accompanied by dismay for the women who either chose to make their living in this fashion or had no other choice.

Now he was feeling nothing short of disgust toward himself. How could he possibly be affected by a public display of crude lustiness?

But affected he was. No matter how many times he pulled his eyes from the dark-haired actress who appeared nude, he couldn't seem to help himself, for his attention was drawn back to her time and again as if by magnetic force. How could he feel such lust for a total stranger? He knew nothing of the woman, save this overwhelming urge to tumble her to the ground, peel the offensive costume from her limbs, and expose her skin in all its soft, feminine glory. To taste her. To take her. To possess her.

He was no better than the other Rose and Thorn members. And for the first time, he got a sense of what his mother's life must have been like. An inkling of why she behaved the way she did.

He shifted his weight from foot to foot, wishing for a cold bath. Damn good thing he was wearing a cloak atop his clothing. He was riveted by the action onstage, notably the place where the dark-haired woman reclined atop the long table. The way she undulated suggestively as each of the other actresses took turns smearing her with stripes of colored paint in an attempt to render her one of them.

Yet, it was obvious to Gray that the woman would never be among the ranks of the others. Something indefinable set her apart. She was part of the group, yet conspicuously alone at the same time. Gray could relate, for there he was, ostensibly one of the Rose and Thorn, yet not.

As the performance drew to an end, the women joined

hands across the front of the stage and took a bow to thunderous, enthusiastic applause. The other actresses took two steps back, leaving the lead actress alone front and center.

Gray felt as if someone had landed him a sharp jab in the solar plexus. He was so stunned by the sudden realization, that at first he couldn't seem to move. His feet felt rooted in place. Slowly, determinedly he regained control and made his way to the front of the crowd and up onto the stage.

Her eyes widened at his approach and she glanced from side to side as if seeking escape, but there was no place she could run. No possible place she could hide.

Gray was so incensed, his hand shook as he reached forward and ripped the dark wig from her head. The light from the lanterns played up the fiery red of Aurora's real hair as it tumbled about her shoulders.

Slowly, she removed her mask and faced him. The audience began to applaud, thinking this was all part of the performance.

Gray flung his cloak at her. "Cover yourself!"

Aurora caught it up but didn't put it on. Instead, she stood holding it, facing him defiantly. "Ever hear the old adage about how the show must go on?"

He snatched back the cloak and covered her with it himself. "This show is over. So is this party."

He jerked her off the stage, through the courtyard, past the ballroom, and into the hallway near the stairs. Aurora had never before seen Grayson well and truly angry as he now pushed her in front of a full-length mirror. "Look at yourself!"

He had a point. She looked cheap and tawdry, covered in

slashes of greasepaint. Her feelings for him were the one thing that was real, but now hardly seemed the right time to tell him as much. "I'm acting a part. Don't you know the difference between real and make-believe?"

"That was no performance. That was sideshow titillation at its lowest."

"Your mother's an actress, I might remind you. She would understand."

"Leave my mother out of this."

"What's the matter, Grayson? Did you get aroused watching me up there? Did you despise yourself and your feelings, because you realize that's how it was for your mother? For the men who saw her onstage and wanted her?"

"Do you enjoy other men gazing at you with lust in their hearts?"

Aurora bit her lip. *Only you,* she'd been about to say. "I never considered myself the type to inspire lust until I met you. I believe the other men simply follow your lead."

"They'll not have you. Only I."

"I thought we established that on first acquaintance."

"Damn you, Aurora." An angry red dot bloomed in each of his cheeks.

"Is that a good 'damn me,' or a bad 'damn me'?"

"You defy me at every turn. And you're not safe here."

"I never was."

Grayson cursed under his breath and turned from her. She'd done it now, Aurora feared. Rendered him too angry for words. She grabbed a cloth napkin from a nearby sideboard, doused it with champagne, and began to scrub the paint from her face. If only she could so easily scrub away the angry feelings she had inspired in Grayson.

Then he was there, before her. He took the bottle of champagne from her hand and drizzled it over her, as if the champagne was a magic elixir, capable of washing away anger and hurt and misunderstandings, to give them both a clean start.

The wine splashed upon her bare shoulders and he licked it off. Kissed it off.

"Grayson . . . ?" Her voice was tremulous. Unsure.

"Ssshhhhh . . ."

He pulled her to him, sheltered her in the circle of his arms, and covered her lips with his own.

Aurora felt as if she might cry just at the taste of his kiss, so sweet and gentle and caring. She let out a shuddery breath as the kiss ended, and blinked away a tear that hovered on her lashes.

"Don't," he said, kissing her eyelids, as if to kiss away the damage and the hurt they had inflicted on each other. "It's as much my fault. I try to control everything and everyone in my life."

"Some things we simply can't control."

"That's not a particularly comfortable feeling for someone whose entire life is based on maintaining control."

At the sound of approaching footsteps they drew apart, as if they had something to be guilty of in their embrace.

"Grayson." Aurora didn't think she could bear for anyone to see her like this.

Grayson seemed privy to her thoughts, for he whisked her into a nearby linen closet and closed the door firmly behind them.

Outside in the hallway there came the sound of a flurry of activity. Indecipherable voices were followed by much scurrying to and fro along the hallway, and the hollow thud of several sets of footsteps up and down the stairs.

Safe in her darkened enclave with Grayson, Aurora was oblivious to all else save him. His warmth. The good clean smell of his skin. The rise and fall of his breath. She took advantage of their close confines to move even closer to him, back to the security of his arms, praying he didn't hate her.

He stood still and unresponsive to her closeness—most of him. The part he couldn't control had a most definite response to her nearness.

"Do you hate me for deceiving you?" she asked.

"Why did you do it?"

"To help out a friend. And because it allowed me to stay here with you."

"I wanted you safely away. I know who killed my father, but I need to trip him up at his own game. I need more time."

"I promise I'll stay out of your way."

"But you can't promise to stay out of my thoughts, can you?"

"Guilty as charged." She leaned into him and somehow in the dark managed to find his lips with her own. She brushed them with hers to feel the inevitable softening, blurring. The way their mouths melded into one as their bodies were also wont to do.

When Grayson started to touch her, she shivered beneath the glory of his caress till he suddenly stopped.

She wasn't accustomed to Grayson's stopping in the middle of anything, particularly something of an intimate nature.

He tugged on the neckline of her costume. "Does this thing have fasteners?"

"It just pulls on and off."

"I'm afraid I'm not that patient."

She heard the sound of tearing cloth, and seconds later the ruined costume lay in shreds around her bare feet.

"Much better," Grayson said, his hands pulling her close.

"You made short work of that," Aurora said. "Did you bring the champagne in with us?"

"I did. Feeling thirsty?"

"No, I just wondered if you wanted any accompaniments while I seduce you."

"You're naked in my arms. That's more than enough seduction for most men."

"Yes, but you're not most men."

She unbuttoned his shirt, pushed it out of the way, and allowed herself the freedom of touching his chest, finding the planes and ridges, the flat male nipples, the crisp matting of hair. She rubbed her breasts against him and felt her body's response, a softening of her limbs, every part of her inside and out growing liquid and moist.

She unfastened his trousers, pushed them out of the way, then knelt before him and took him into her mouth. She loved his smooth, hard length. The way his breath caught. She rolled her tongue around him, end to end, added a deep, satisfying pull for good measure, then rose.

"Aurora." Her name on his lips had never sounded so seductive.

She wrapped her arms around his shoulders as she wrapped her legs around his waist. He caught her beneath her bottom, supported her weight as her heat sought and found his, greedy and impatient.

He teased her, rubbing himself against her as if poised for possession, then pulled away, laughing at her soft moan of frustration.

"Grayson." Gently she pummeled his shoulders with her fists. "Don't tease me so, you wretch."

"You want this?" Slowly he began to ease his cock inside her.

She moaned deeply as she felt his penetration, slow and sure and filling her completely. Her body throbbed and welcomed him inside her, sheathing him in her velvet heat.

"Oh, yes!" Head thrown back, eyes closed, she moved with him, against him, her frenzied rhythm meeting and matching his. Slower. Faster. Then slow again, which gave her opportunity to reach down and touch them both.

"I love it when you do that," Grayson said, his words labored as he continued to meet and match her rhythm.

"What? Touch you?" Aurora asked, ringing him with her thumb and forefinger. "Or touch myself?"

"Touch us both. Increase our pleasure."

"Your wish is my command."

Intensity grew in their coupling as someone bumped into the door from the other side. At any second the door could be flung open, leading to their discovery. The risk and excitement added a frenzied exhilaration that fueled their pace. She could hear the sound of her bottom slapping against Grayson's thighs as she met and matched his powerful thrusts. She reached down to fondle his balls, then in a sudden flash of daring, slid her baby finger around to stimulate his nether opening. He caught his breath and hugged her hard, seeming to enjoy the unexpectedness of her move. Further emboldened, she slid her baby finger inside him the way he had done to her. He found her mouth in the dark, kissed her deeply, approvingly. Did she imagine it, or did he grow even harder, deepening the penetration, increasing the pleasure beyond all comprehension?

Release, when it finally came, was as swift and as all-consuming as the urgency with which they made love. Aurora muffled her scream of ecstasy against Grayson's neck at the same moment he shuddered and emptied himself into her.

Slowly, still cradled against him, she unwrapped her legs and found her feet. She leaned weakly against him, enjoying the loving way he smoothed the length of her spine and followed the soft curve of her backside.

"That was one damn fine walling," he whispered, his breath ragged against her perspiration-dampened forehead. "Still, I think I prefer the softness of a bed."

"I know where we can find one," she said, her arms still wrapped around him for support. "Think the coast is clear now?"

"It's quieted down. Best we make a dash for it." As he straightened his clothing, Aurora wrapped herself from head to toe in his cloak. He opened the door, gave her the all-clear sign, and whisked her up the stairs to her room.

They burst inside, Aurora giggling at the silliness of their antics. At the look on Grayson's face, her laughter died in her throat. Belatedly, she realized the room was warm and well lit. And currently occupied by its rightful owner.

"Hello, Mother," Grayson said. "What brings you out this way?"

Chapter Twelve

Aurora huddled inside Gray's cloak, keenly aware of her state of undress and the fact that mere moments earlier she and Grayson had been in the throes of—

She couldn't think about that now. Not when Celeste Grayson stood on the far side of the room, as magnificently in command of her audience as ever.

Aurora recalled the time when they'd worked together; the way there had been no blurring of reality and fantasy for the stage diva. No shift from one world to the other, the way things did for Aurora. She was certain that was what made the woman such an amazing stage presence. Acting was not Celeste's work. Acting was her.

"Well, well." Celeste looked her up and down imperially. "And might this happen to be who's been sleeping in my bed?"

Aurora would have given anything to fade invisible, but Grayson drew her forward. "Aurora, allow me to present my mother, Celeste Grayson. Mother, Aurora Tremblay is our guest this weekend. And yes, I did assign her your room in your absence."

Celeste cocked a brow in amusement. "A move that tells me more than you will ever possibly know, Gray." She directed her attention back to Aurora. "You look familiar. If memory serves, we've acted together, have we not?"

"I'm honored that you would remember me," Aurora said.

"Believe me. In this business, it pays to remember everyone, friend or foe."

"I'm sorry for my intrusion," Aurora said, edging sideways. "I'll just collect up my things and . . ." Her words trailed away. She could hardly verbalize the rest of her thought. *Get out of here and get some clothing on.*

"Speaking of foes," Grayson said easily.

"You need not say another word. I have eyes. I must tell you, Grayson, I never thought I'd see the day the Rose and Thorn would be installed here on the estate." Her voice rose dramatically. "I feel your grandparents, even now, rolling over in their graves."

"Father was an active member in the club."

"But he never brought it home with him. Home was always neutral."

Grayson laughed humorlessly. "Neutral. That's hardly the way I recall my youth."

"A fact for which you blame me, I'm certain. Just remember, things are never exactly as they appear."

"No. Everything with you was always an act."

"Not everything. I loved your father till the day he died."

"And you and I both know there is no way Father would choose to end his own life."

Celeste nodded in agreement. "A mortal sin of the worst possible degree. Jonathan would never risk eternity in hell."

"Is that why you two stayed married? Because of the Church?"

"We stayed married because it suited us both. I admit, the way we chose to honor our marriage vows would not be for everyone, electing to enjoy a certain level of freedom within the confines of our marriage."

"Then why marry at all?"

Was it Aurora's imagination, or did Celeste flush? "Because it suited us. Now, where is your brother? I sent for him when I first arrived at the estate."

"Beau has his own agenda, Mother. He'll show up when it suits him and not a second sooner."

"Yes, I fear Beau didn't inherit your innate sense of responsibility." She narrowed her gaze thoughtfully. "On the other hand, I've often thought perhaps you received his measure along with your own."

Once more Aurora found herself on the receiving end of that assessing gaze, so like Grayson's. "From what I recall, Aurora, you're also not the type to embrace the Rose and Thorn Club and their antics."

"Not at all," Aurora admitted.

"Yet you were onstage tonight. I caught part of the performance."

"I was standing in for a friend."

"I admire loyalty. I knew your parents. They were both highly admirable people."

"Thank you," Aurora said. "I miss them very much."

Celeste turned to Grayson. "Why don't you run along and attend to whatever it is that has you so fidgety, Gray? Leave us two girls to catch up on old theater gossip."

"That suits me perfectly. I have several loose ends that require a tight knot."

Aurora watched Grayson's retreat with a strong sense of foreboding. Whatever he was about, she longed to be part of it, not tucked away like some ineffectual ninny, chatting and drinking tea with his mother.

"I'm sure you'll be more comfortable once you put on some clothes, dear."

Aurora blushed deeply. How had the woman known she was naked beneath her cloak?

Celeste smiled. "Don't be embarrassed. Grayson is very much his father's son. More than a time or two, I found myself in a compromising position with Jonathan." She sighed dramatically. "I miss him very much. I expect one day Grayson will figure out just why Jonathan and I got married. Now, why exactly are you here seducing my son?"

Aurora bristled at the implication. "I'm hardly anyone's seductress. I'm attempting to convince Grayson not to tear down the Gaslight Theater. I'd hoped either to buy or lease it from him. It's an ideal site for showing moving pictures. And I have a fond attachment for the building."

"Very entrepreneurial of you, my dear. I also foresee a day when many of us in this business will act for film as well as onstage."

"Grayson doesn't share my view."

"Gray blames that theater for all that went wrong with our family. Far easier than blaming me or his father."

"Yet I hold it dear for all that went right with mine."

"A balanced view is important. I predict that together, you and Grayson will make a strong and complementary team."

"I'm doing my best to convince him of that very thing. A business venture," she added hastily.

Celeste's eyes rolled to the heavens. "Sons. A mother's great joy and infinite challenge. Why couldn't I have a nice, easy-to-understand daughter instead of my two difficult and moody boys?" She laughed. "Except I love them both dearly and can't imagine my life without them."

"Perhaps it wouldn't be a bad idea to tell them as much. To make sure they're aware of the fact." Aurora smiled at the image. The legendary Celeste Grayson holding court, the imperial majesty reigning love down upon her loyal subjects.

Maybe once Celeste was done telling Grayson she loved him, it would be Aurora's turn. Maybe Grayson would come to realize love wasn't such a scary thing. That the love of a woman, be it she or his mother, needn't render him weak and helpless.

"He wasn't very happy to see me onstage tonight."

"They never are, my dear. Respect the art, suspect the

artist. His father was exactly the same. He'll come around. Jonathan always did." She sighed. "In spite of our differences, his was the greatest love, the greatest passion I ever experienced."

"More than the stage?"

"The love I held for Jonathan was second to none."

"You should tell that to Grayson, too."

"That's one of the reasons I'm here. Jonathan could rant and rave with the best of them, but in the end he was totally supportive. Even though he wasn't Beau's father." She sighed. "The things we do in an attempt to protect the ones we love."

The comment gave Aurora pause. Is that what Grayson was doing with her? Trying to protect her? Did that mean perhaps he loved her, as well?

"I'll always regret the night I drank too much and told Jonathan the truth—how Julian forced himself on me, with Beau as the result. John was furious that I hadn't told him right away. Yet those two were always so close, like brothers. How could I be the one to tear them apart?"

The door flew open to reveal Beau standing on the other side. His face was thunderous as he made his way toward them. "No wonder you love Gray more than you love me."

"Beau." Celeste looked stricken. She extended a hand to him but he shook it off. "That's not true. I love you both equally."

"How could you love me? How could anyone?"

"Nothing is so bad when it gave me you, son."

"At least I know now why you kept my parentage from me. I always did wonder, you know." As he spoke, Beau fidgeted with the ring on his left hand like a young man hauled up before the headmaster. Aurora's eyes widened. Beau wore the broken Rose and Thorn ring, just as Misty had said.

Did that mean . . . ? Was it possible . . . ? Could Beau have killed Jonathan Thorne in an attempt to learn the identity of his own father?

"Gray always gave me what-for, saying I spoiled you when you were younger. I fear he may have been correct on that count."

"Funny. I'm starting to believe Gray was right about a lot of things," Beau said.

"You always did look up to him," Celeste said softly. "I loved to watch you as you followed him around."

Beau got a strange and thoughtful look on his face, as if he was someplace other than in the room with Aurora and his mother. "Sometimes the truth, no matter how bad it may seem, is kinder than the things our minds concoct."

"Beau." Celeste reached out an entreating hand. Too late, for Beau slammed out of the room.

"Let me talk to him," Aurora said, as she turned and raced after him. Already he was out of sight, but she could hear his footfalls on the stairs ahead of her. She clasped the railing and hastened to catch up before the noise of the party drowned him out.

GRAY STRODE DOWN the hallway, bellowing for Randall as he went. Randall skidded around a corner, and the two men barely managed to avoid colliding.

"Where the hell is Julian?" Gray asked.

"I don't know."

"I thought I told you to watch him."

"I *was* watching him. He was quite interested in the dressing-down you gave Aurora in front of everyone. But with the way your guests were milling about, he managed to give me the slip."

"Find him," Gray barked, "and bring him to my study. He has quite a number of things to answer for. Beginning with forging my father's signature on the mortgage for the theater."

"I'll try. But I have to warn you, the crowd is going wild. Finding Julian in this melee will be quite difficult."

"Get Beau to help you. It's well past time he did his part around here."

"Forgive me, but I thought you preferred keeping Beau at a distance."

True—he'd deliberately kept everyone at a distance. A fact that somehow, because of Aurora, had recently changed. "Tell him I said it was well past time he involved himself in this family. All aspects of it."

"Right-o!" Randall made a smart salute and swung about to do Gray's bidding.

THE KITCHEN WAS DARK and deserted. Ahead of her, Beau had slowed his pace, and Aurora adjusted hers accordingly, allowing her eyes to grow accustomed to the lack of light. She had no desire to bang into something and alert Beau to her presence.

He disappeared through a narrow doorway she had never seen before. She waited a few seconds, then followed. The dark, rickety staircase led below the kitchen into what had to be a cellar. She clung to the handrail and prayed the stairs were sound, as she couldn't see a thing in front of her.

Eventually her feet struck dirt instead of wood, and she took a breath. It was cool, the smell damp and earthy. She could just make out the faint flicker of light up ahead, and proceeded toward it cautiously.

They were in the wine cellar, she realized, as she passed between rows of dusty bottles stored on their sides. As she approached the light, she could hear the low murmur of men's voices. Cautiously she edged forward and crouched behind a barrel. By peering around the side of it she could just make out two shadowy figures. Beau stood with his back to her, face-to-face with Julian.

The two men stood like dogs getting each other's scent. The similarity in their stance was so obvious, she had to stifle her gasp of recognition.

"Did you bring your brother's ring?" the older man asked.

As Beau raised his hand, candlelight glinted on the silver. "How did it get broken?" he asked.

"There was a slight accident," Julian said.

"Gray doesn't have accidents."

"Quite right, my boy. Quite right on that score."

"So this isn't Gray's ring."

"Quite right again. Perhaps you're not as stupid as your mother, after all."

"And not as unconscionable as my father."

"Whoever that unfortunate gent may be."

Beau advanced. "Oh, I think you know. I think you know

perfectly well who sired me. Even if you never wanted to accept responsibility for your actions."

"Is that what she told you, then? It's all lies. You see, I don't choose to share my conquests. And your mother was always rather free with her favors."

Aurora stifled her gasp as Beau lashed out to hit Julian. Julian had been obviously expecting just such a response, for from behind his back he produced a stout wooden club. Aurora saw movement, started forward to help, then froze as the club connected with the back of Beau's skull with a dull thud. She heard Beau's body slump to the packed-dirt floor of the cellar and watched Julian bend down and wrest the ring from the young man's limp hand. He straightened and tucked the ring in his inside jacket pocket. Aurora scooted back behind her barrel, but not quick enough. Julian must have caught the flash of movement, for he turned very slowly and deliberately in her direction.

Light and shadow heightened the menace in his stance as he took a step forward. His grip tightened on the club, and his gaze shifted from side to side. He had no way of knowing how many people were there, hidden in the shadows, and Aurora saw uncertainty cross his features, replaced by steely determination.

"Who's there? Step forward this moment before I lose my patience."

Aurora glanced around seeking a weapon, anything she could use to defend herself against the man. She grabbed a dust-shrouded wine bottle and tucked it beneath her cloak before inching farther into the shadows.

"So that's it, then," Julian said, his voice deepening in anticipation. "I always do enjoy a round of hide-and-seek." He licked his lips. His nose twitched like a hound scenting a fox. "You know, of course, there's no way out."

Aurora was studying her surroundings, wondering if she could somehow creep around and come out in back of him. She kept him in sight as she silently edged past the stacked-up barrels, only to reach a dead end.

"Come out, come out, wherever you are." Julian's singsong voice made her skin crawl. She couldn't stay here, cornered. Nothing for it but to confront him and hope surprise was on her side.

"There are far more pleasant spots on the estate for a liaison," she said casually as she stepped forward to reveal herself.

"Well, well, well," Julian said with a sinister chuckle. "What have we here? Not Grayson's latest obsession? And all alone in the bargain."

"What makes you think I'm alone?"

"I've been watching you the entire time. I know you're alone."

"You might as well give it up," Aurora said bravely. "Grayson knows you killed his father." As she moved into the dim circle of light, she cast an anxious glance at Beau's unmoving form.

Julian correctly interpreted her look. "Not to worry, my dear. He'll come to later with a headache, but I have no intention of killing my own offspring. In fact, I believe the young buck will be quite useful to me. If Gray hasn't left him the estate, I'll simply arrange to have the will changed."

"I suppose that's been your plan all along?"

Julian sighed heavily, as if aggrieved by her words. "I find it's far better not to make long-term plans, but to seize the opportunity when one presents itself. Like now." When he stepped forward she held her ground, even as his eyes slid over her cloaked figured in an insinuating way.

"Move forward, my dear. Let me drink in your beauty."

"I prefer distance between us."

"You'll soon change your tune. They all do." He closed the gap, grasped her chin between thumb and forefinger, and pinched.

"Stop that." Aurora pushed his hand away. "You're hurting me."

His face lit up with a sinister pleasure. "Consider it a small prelude of what's to come."

"I know you're the one who beat up Misty."

"That's a rather harsh assessment of our sexual escapades."

Aurora had to keep him talking, distract him till he let down his guard. "You enjoy hurting people."

"Yes, inflicting pain is one of my many pleasures."

"Is that why you started the club with Grayson's father?"

"No. Not at all," Julian said. "The club was strictly a business decision on my part. Unfortunately, Jonathan didn't always approve of my business practices. Simply because I forged his signature on the mortgage for the theater . . . I mean, we were both equal partners. Sometimes one partner is forced to do something the other one dislikes."

"Your ring got broken in the theater that day. So you switched rings with Grayson."

"My, but you have been busy. I confess I have long delighted in taking things that belong to the Thorne family. I enjoyed taking Celeste from Jonathan." He grew thoughtful. "Silly Jonathan. Rather late to be confronting me, intent on defending the honor of his wife. As if that woman had any honor worth left defending."

"Is that why he was killed?"

He seemed to relax slightly, warming to his subject. "I'd like to say it was an accident. But truly, in life, there are no accidents."

Aurora's grasp tightened on the neck of the wine bottle. Would one blow be enough to knock him out? She had to make sure it counted. Wait till he was in the exact right position . . .

"One thing I always admired about you is your air of power." She reached out to touch his hand, trying to angle her body and widen her stance. She started to bring the bottle into position, but Julian caught her slight movement.

"What's this then?" Julian grasped her wrist and twisted, hard enough to bring tears to her eyes, and she was forced to let go. The bottle landed on the ground near her feet.

Julian kicked it aside, his eyes widening and spittle forming at the corner of his mouth as he saw bare skin. "My, my. You've been taking your cues from fair Celeste. She always used her body to bewitch the men in exactly the same way."

He flicked back a panel of the cloak, and Aurora shrank from his gaze, for she'd had no time to dress in her haste to follow Beau.

"Now, you look to be a woman ready for some fun. And

guess what? A damp, musty cellar is one of my favorite settings." He edged in closer, pawing her bare arm. "No one will hear you scream if things should happen to get a little rough for your tastes." He punctuated his words with an unpleasant laugh. "This is one little tryst I'm going to particularly enjoy."

"You'll not get away with it."

"I don't see anyone here to stop me, do you?"

"That depends on where you're looking."

Aurora started at the welcome sound of Grayson's voice. He strolled into plain view, a revolver held steady in his right hand, aimed straight for Julian's heart. Julian still had hold of Aurora, and before she could blink, he snapped her around in front of himself as a shield.

"You won't be taking a shot at me, Grayson. Not as long as there's a chance you could miss me and hit your lovely lady here."

Grayson's voice was calm. "Are you all right, Aurora?"

"I'm fine. But he knocked Beau out."

Grayson took a step forward.

Julian backed up, dragging Aurora with him. "Move back from the stairs, Grayson. I'm getting out of here and taking her with me."

"And where, I wonder, do you think you're going? I have evidence that will see you locked up, with the key thrown away forever. You embezzled from my father's business, then killed him."

"Your father was a weak man."

Aurora could feel the harsh rise and fall of Julian's breath against the back of her neck. His arm was like a vise across her middle, trapping her against him.

"My father wasn't perfect, by any means. But he was a far better man than you are."

"You don't know the escapades we got into in our youth. Everything was perfect until he met her. Celeste. She changed him. And after that, nothing was the same."

"Love changes people, Julian. Something you'd not be familiar with, not being capable of love yourself."

Love had certainly changed her life, Aurora thought. And she'd tell Grayson that if she ever got the chance.

"Let Aurora go. I'll give you a head start."

"You think I'm stupid? I'll not get off this estate without her as my trump card." When Julian started to edge toward the stairs, Aurora dug in her feet and went limp in his grasp, to no avail. He dragged her with him as if she were a bundle of rags.

All of a sudden he tripped, and started to go down.

Aurora took advantage of his loosening grip to dive out of the way.

"Now, Grayson!" she shouted.

A shot rang out. She felt the bullet whiz past her. Heard Julian's cry of pain and saw him stagger backward, his hand over his thigh, stained red with blood.

As Aurora scrambled on all fours to safety, she saw Beau had regained consciousness and his hand was firmly clutching Julian's ankle.

"Well done, Beau," Grayson said.

Beau rose unsteadily to his feet, picked up a nearby length of rope, and approached where Julian lay, holding fast to his gunshot wound as if to stem the tide of blood. "You're into bondage," he told Julian. "This should be right up your alley."

"I need medical attention. Don't leave me here to bleed to death. You're my son!"

"That's nothing I'll ever admit to. And I expect you'll survive to face the magistrate."

Grayson helped Aurora to her feet. She reached toward him; she had so much to tell him.

"You do tend to rush in where angels would stay away."

She stiffened at his words and wrapped her arms protectively about her middle. "Since I have no intention of changing, please don't bother to lecture me."

"Don't go getting all prickly on me." His arm clasped her shoulder, comfortably possessive. "I would never lecture you, my dear. For I fully expect our future adventures together will be anything but dull."

She turned to him. Did he say "future"? She had no chance to inquire, for after that, everything seemed to happen at once. Randall showed up with a local law officer who had been on-site all weekend. After ensuring Beau was all right and Julian was carted away, Grayson bundled Aurora upstairs and into his bed, where she fell into a long, deep sleep.

The sun was high by the time she woke the next morning, alone. She found Grayson on the verandah, dressed to travel.

"Are you going somewhere?"

"Only if it suits you." Puzzled, she followed his gaze. A tiny speck in the sky gradually drew closer, and she saw it was a hot-air balloon.

She glanced askance at Grayson, who was smiling as she'd never seen him smile before.

"Before you say a word, hear me out. I told you the other day I had no intention of selling you the theater. That much was true. What I failed to disclose is that I was in the process of paying off the mortgage and transferring the property to your name, as a betrothal gift. Assuming you agree to be my wife."

He kissed her lightly, almost hesitantly. "If you don't wish to marry me, I shall have to think of some other means to pass the theater to your hands. But this way seemed the simplest by far."

"A betrothal gift? For me to do with as I wish?"

"Whatever your heart desires."

"My heart desires you above all else."

He smiled. "Thank goodness for that. For I was about to make quite the nuisance of myself following you about the country, attempting to convince you of the depth of my love."

She pretended to consider his words. "That sounds like fun. How soon will we get started?"

He indicated to where the balloon was setting down on the manicured lawn below them. "How about now?"

"You're serious?"

"I thought to take a leaf from the life of a woman I know, one who claims herself to be a grand adventuress. We'll make this the start of a whole new adventure—our life together."

Aurora's blood thundered through her veins in anticipation. Still, she pretended to consider his offer. "Where will we go?"

"Whichever way the wind blows."

The perfect answer! Aurora leaned into him, awash in the

rightness of him by her side forever. "I must confess, I have a hankering to make love in a hot-air balloon."

"In that case, one of us will need to learn to pilot the thing, so we have some privacy."

"Why not both of us?"

"Why not, indeed?" He kissed her long and hard, sealing their contract.

As they set off, Beau, Randall, and Celeste stood on the lawn waving good-bye. After she watched them gradually growing smaller and smaller in the distance, Aurora turned to smile up at Grayson, secure in his embrace. "Isn't life indeed a grand adventure?"

He tightened his hold in agreement. "I have a feeling our adventures together have only just begun."